DANGER IN THE WINGS

Geoffrey Trease was born in 1909, and has always loved writing and history. His first children's novel, *Bows against the Barons*, published in 1934, combined the two. He is now the highly acclaimed author of over one hundred books for children and a number of adult works, including novels and a history of London. He has been published in twenty languages.

Having travelled widely in Europe, lived in Russia and served in India during the Second World War, Geoffrey Trease now lives in Bath, close to his daughter, a college lecturer, and is in constant touch with his four granddaughters and his great-grandchildren.

DANGER
IN THE
WINGS

Geoffrey Trease

Hodder Children's Books

a division of Hodder Headline plc

First published in Great Britain in 1997
by Hodder Children's Books

10 9 8 7 6 5 4 3 2 1

A Catalogue record for this book is available from the
British Library

Hardback ISBN 0 340 68167 5
Paperback ISBN 0 340 68168 3

Typeset by Avon Dataset Ltd, Bidford-on-Avon, Warks
Printed and bound in Great Britain by
Mackays of Chatham PLC, Chatham, Kent

Hodder Children's Books
A division of Hodder Headline plc
338 Euston Road
London NW1 3BH

For James and Joanna and Sophie

One

In those first heart-stopping moments – he always remembered afterwards – the course of his whole life must have been decided.

It was when he saw the ghost.

The tension had started with his earliest glimpse of those shadowy battlements and the sharp cry of the sentry: 'Who's there?' But the climax came with that uncanny figure, glinting like silver in the dark.

It happened, of course, in New York. It could not have occurred at home in Boston. That was why Dan, as soon as his ship docked in the Hudson river, had hurried eagerly ashore for his first evening alone in a strange city.

He had inquired for the theatre. Boston (which prided itself on having everything) had no theatre. New York was one of the few towns in the American colonies that did.

He was directed to John Street. 'It's off Broadway,' said a helpful docker. Broadway proved to be quite narrow. He found John Street and the theatre which had been opened only five years before.

Tonight the play was Shakespeare's *Hamlet*. He was in luck. Though he had never set foot in a playhouse he knew what happened in that exciting drama. The plots and murders, the poisoned drink and the poisoned rapier-point in the duel, the tragic drowning – was it really suicide? – of the beautiful Ophelia. Boston had great respect for Shakespeare. You could read his work in print, you could hear it recited in public and lectured about by famous men.

In fact, Dan told himself as he took his seat in the theatre pit, he knew a lot that even Hamlet himself at this moment did not.

The Danish prince had been far away at a German university when he'd heard of his father's sudden mysterious death. Hurrying back for the funeral he had been met with another shock. The queen, his mother, was going to marry his uncle Claudius – immediately. Only now, when he met his father's ghost on the battlements, was he to hear the facts.

If Dan had felt any superiority from his own inside knowledge, it vanished when the curtain rose. He was gripped from the first moment. He had read these words before, but it was so different when they were spoken. The sentry's challenge, the terse replies, the contemptuous disbelief of Hamlet's friend Horatio, the electrifying interruption by Marcellus, 'Peace! Break thee off! Look where it comes again!' And there, indeed, it came. Stalking silently across the stage.

Not speaking a word. It would not speak till Hamlet himself was there to hear. The cock crowed and the ghost in gleaming armour departed. Then fresh chandeliers were drawn across, the stage became bright gold with candlelight, and the murderous King Claudius entered with his courtiers.

Dan sat forward eagerly. This acting made all the difference. It was spellbinding.

He remembered one of his parents' dinner-parties. A pompous guest, a real goody-goody, had scoffed at the idea that Boston should have a theatre, like Philadelphia, New York and Williamsburg. 'We have the poet's immortal words, we can read and discuss them ourselves. We do not need a *playhouse* – hotbed of scandal! We do not want one anywhere in Massachusetts!'

Dan had longed to say (but it was not for a schoolboy to speak,) 'Surely Shakespeare *wrote* his plays to be acted?'

Tonight he knew why.

It was not just the words but the way they were spoken – the tone, the timing, the gestures, the expression on the actor's face. Oh, so many things. The way you could suggest emotion or a quite different thought behind the literal meaning. What an art! Were actors taught it? Or did they have to work it all out for themselves?

If you *could* do it, how wonderful it must be. To set a whole audience rocking with laughter! Or to check it in an instant and produce a pin-drop silence! To bring a howl of disgust, a murmur of sympathy, a roar of approval . . . What must it feel like to wield such power?

The play went on, scene after scene that he remembered but now saw transformed. Silly old Polonius died, deservedly, as he eavesdropped behind the curtain. Poor Ophelia went mad. The strolling players tricked Claudius into betraying his guilt. Claudius plotted the duel, to eliminate his awkward nephew. Shakespeare had certainly written all this to be acted . . .

When an interval came, Dan resented it and was eager to continue. A chatty gentleman beside him started a conversation. Dan would have preferred to spend those minutes lost in a dream of Denmark long ago. But he had to remember his manners and answer. Explain that it was his first visit to New York, that he was the youngest son of John Carnaby, the well-known ship-owner.

The conversation, however, proved interesting.

'It's an English company,' said the stranger. 'We depend mainly on these acting companies that sail over from England.' There were so few people yet in the colonies who had taken up acting as a living. 'It's quite an art, my boy.' Dan did not need to be told.

'I remember the very first company Lewis Hallam brought over. That's going back more than twenty years! 1750. Then a Mr David Douglass took over from him. They did *King Lear, Romeo and Juliet, Merchant of Venice* – other men's work, too. But you can't beat Shakespeare.'

At first, the English companies had to act in makeshift halls and even barns, but soon proper theatres began to spring up. 'This is our third effort in New York – five years it's been going. With luck, I reckon it will survive—'

'Oh, it deserves to, sir!'

The musicians stopped playing, a single trumpet sounded, the chatter was stilled. They were back in the haunted castle of Elsinore . . . The tragedy swept on to its terrible climax, the stage was strewn with bodies. Hamlet himself gasped out his closing lines: 'I die Horatio. The potent poison quite o'ecrows my spirit. I cannot live to hear the news from England—'

Five minutes later Dan found himself in the street outside, saying a polite good-night to the talkative stranger, who inquired anxiously if Dan was sure he could find the place where his ship was moored.

'Oh, yes, thank you, sir. I know my way back.'

But at that moment he could have said, just as truthfully, that he also knew his way forward.

Two

Later, at home in Boston, the Carnaby family questioned Dan. What had he enjoyed most on his trip?

He needed no encouragement. He plunged into an enthusiastic account of that first visit to a theatre. He described the two very different plays he had seen. The ship was docked for four days, one of which, alas, was a Sunday. Otherwise he could have fitted in a third play. The actors were wonderful, they changed their programmes constantly.

The family listened politely, but showed obvious relief at a change of subject.

No, said Dan apologetically, he could not recall the name of the church he had attended, or give them an outline of the hour-long sermon. His mother and his brothers were keener to hear more of his impressions of New York. His father was still keener to know his reactions to life aboard ship. 'How was it?' he inquired.

Dan tried to be tactful. 'I was treated very well – splendid little cabin – all the crew most helpful.'

'Do you wonder?' said his brother George. 'Boss's son!'

'I was most emphatic,' said Mr Carnaby. 'No favours.'

'You weren't seasick?' asked Mrs Carnaby anxiously.

'Oh no, Mother. Only sometimes sick of the sea!'

His father looked sad. 'You were bored?'

'It was better when we sailed close in,' Dan said hastily, 'and saw the coast. You get tired of just looking at water all the time.'

'Didn't Captain Briggs show you the chart-room, as I'd asked? Talk to you about navigation?'

'He went to great pains, Father. But you know I was always stupid about mathematics. I'm better with words than numbers. They're not *human* enough.'

His eldest brother Thomas chuckled. 'I expect there was something missing. No gals on a ship.'

Their mother exploded with indignation. 'What would Dan be wanting with *girls*?' Nobody tried to answer that.

Mr Carnaby got back to his own line of thought. 'Maybe I made a mistake,' he said. 'When you came to my office I realised it was not the place for you. Your brothers seemed happy enough. I doubted if you would be. There is—' he hesitated.

'A streak of the adventurer in you.' Dan took this as a compliment, but was surprised that his father had gained such an impression. 'Do not misunderstand me. A boy should be making up his mind what he wants to do in the world. I don't expect all my sons to help me in my business. There would be a place for you, if you chose . . .'

'Thank you, Father.'

'It need not mean life in the counting-house. We have ships. We trade all over the world. I thought that side might appeal to you. Not a desk, but a deck. I sent you on this little coastal trip just to New York. Perhaps I should have given you something more adventurous. We have ships going to the West Indies – or over to England and France and Holland. Even wild places in Africa, like Guinea.' He smiled across the supper table. 'You have only to say the word. I could fix it. If you liked it, you could learn – work your way up – one day even command your own vessel. See the world.'

A month ago Dan might have been tempted. Not now. He fumbled for polite words. He admired his father and was grateful. Not many boys had a father like his. But even the patient Mr Carnaby could not wait forever. He cut through his son's floundering. 'Is there anything else you would *like* to do? Just tell us.'

What a god-send, that invitation!

Dan licked his dry lips. 'Since you ask, Father, I would like to be a play-actor.'

There were gasps round the table. He could not have surprised them more if he had said 'buffalo' or 'octopus' instead.

'*What?*'

'Are they properly paid? Could you earn a living?'

'Is it a *respectable* occupation?' His mother suddenly became rather grand. 'Is it something a member of a family like ours – a Carnaby–'

Thomas and George agreed for once. New York had turned the kid's head. Their two married brothers were not there, but Dan knew they would have said the same.

Only his father managed to consider his announcement sensibly. 'I must admit, Dan, you have me at a disadvantage. I've no idea how to advise you. Or what I could do to help. It's unknown territory to me. I don't know whom to ask. Nobody in Boston–'

Usually his father knew somebody – somebody with knowledge and influence – whatever the problem. But who in Boston knew anything about matters theatrical?

'I thought of that. I thought, while we were in New York, I'd better try to see the theatre manager.'

'Now that was sensible! What did he say?'

'He was very kind. But not very encouraging.'

'Thank God,' Dan heard his mother murmur.

'If you've no family connections, you try to get into a company – take on the humblest job backstage, get tried out in small parts, learn as you go, try to show you have a talent. That's how it is in England. But in the colonies there are so few theatres, and we haven't the companies. That's why these English companies come over on tour—'

'A difficult business. I see that.' His father sounded almost sympathetic. 'How wise to inquire while you had the chance! Lucky this man was hard-headed and laid the facts before you, even if it meant disappointing you.'

'I'm not disappointed. It just means—' Dan looked his father straight in the eye. 'I must go to England.'

'England?' His mother sounded utterly horrified. 'All that way?'

He swung round and faced her. 'The same distance as if I was sailing with cargoes for Carnaby's! You would not worry if it was Madagascar – if *Dad* wanted me to.'

'But you would come back!' she wailed.

'And I shall come back from England – once I've learnt the trade. By then, we might have a theatre even here.'

'Or you'll start one,' Thomas mocked him.

Their mother tried to muster arguments against his folly. 'But would you be happy in such work? It's one thing to enjoy these play-actors in the theatre. But to be one of them? To have to remember all those lines, though I know how good you were at school. The master himself said you were the best of the bunch. And all the dressing up in strange clothes, and passing yourself off as someone completely different—'

Dan laughed. 'You forget, Mother. I was at the Tea Party!'

'Perhaps that is something it would be better to forget,' said his father. 'I was all in sympathy with its objects. But it was shockingly illegal – not something for a respectable Carnaby to get mixed up in. If you'd asked my permission beforehand to take part—'

'That's why I didn't, Dad!'

The Boston Tea Party was now famous. One day it would be history. Dan had been drawn into it with one or two other senior boys at his school.

12

For years the thirteen colonies had been resentful that their affairs were run by a British government across the Atlantic. Even respectable Boston citizens like Mr Carnaby shared in the indignation. 'I have nothing against England,' he would say. 'My own grandparents and my wife's grandparents came from England. But why should this king – who's more German than English anyhow – consider himself our king, too? And fix the taxes we have to pay?'

The taxes got under everyone's skin, especially the new tea tax. It had caused a tremendous outcry. Protest meetings, demonstrations, a popular movement against drinking tea. Three English vessels had been moored in Boston harbour with cargoes of tea that the dockers refused to unload.

That led to the Tea Party.

Dan and his friends, eager for excitement, had joined the demonstrators raiding the ships. To avoid recognition, and being arrested, they had all dressed up as Mohawk Indians, with feathered headdresses and faces daubed with war paint. They had swarmed over the three vessels. The outnumbered seamen were either deceived by their disguise or secretly sympathetic to their cause. Over three hundred chests of tea were thrown overboard and still lay at the bottom of the harbour.

Dan remembered the adventure with glee. But he did not seriously think that acting as an Indian that day would help him in his dream of a theatrical career.

Once more his father brought the conversation back to the matter in hand. 'You may be crazy,' he said. 'But I can do nothing but admire your determination.'

'You can, Father,' Dan corrected him.

'Such as what?'

'Give me a free passage on your next ship going to Bristol. And a letter of introduction to the man you deal with there – Mr Widdowson, isn't it?'

'You are a mighty persuasive boy. But matters like these have to be considered at leisure.' Father rose from his chair. The debate was adjourned.

The scene Dan had dreaded had gone better than he dared to hope. A good first act, he told himself. With luck, the final curtain would bring him the ending he wanted.

Three

There were endless family arguments that week.

Dan's brothers agreed that the kid was crazy. Mother was full of misgivings, sometimes tearful, sometimes exasperated. Father, as always, was fair-minded and cautiously sympathetic.

None of them had ever set foot in a theatre. They could not imagine those evenings in New York or 'understand what had got into the boy'. Father knew no more than any of them.

'But I have never been to Africa,' he pointed out. 'I guessed – and I've been proved right – that there's business to be done there.'

'But Daniel is not Africa!'

'True, my dear.'

'He is young, he could get into difficulties!'

'Also true.'

Father was like a rock, too solid to budge. He believed in independence, even for sons. Dan must have a chance. 'We are always taking chances in our business, my dear. One has to with ships. I shall give the boy a modest allowance – for six months, say. Widdowson will arrange it for us with an English bank—'

'For six months!'

'We don't know how this play-acting business is run. I don't suppose one can find work straight off. We can afford it. Then, if he cannot make his way, he must come home.'

As a ship-owner, Father had got used to losing money occasionally on a venture that had not paid off. Maybe, thought Dan, he had a secret idea that a longer, more interesting Atlantic voyage would remove his son's objections to a career at sea. But it won't, he vowed. True, he had moments of doubt about possible failure in this unknown, now rather frightening, world ahead, but he pushed them away.

He made the crossing late in the summer. A good time to go, before the autumn gales. It was also the season, he had learnt in New York, when theatres made their winter plans.

Carnaby's did much of their business with Bristol, the second largest port in Britain. Whereas London faced the other way, Bristol looked west to America, which saved on sailing time and wages.

'Time is money,' Dan's father used to say.

That was why he liked schooners. They were

fast and needed only a small crew (saving money, again). And their cargo capacity was excellent. Dan skimmed swiftly across the Atlantic on the pleasant August breeze.

Was there a theatre in Bristol? Nobody seemed certain. Theatres came and went. They were chancey ventures still, even in England – and Ireland too, though play-going was popular in Dublin.

Dan warned himself to be prepared for setbacks.

He could do one thing to prepare himself. He spent hours in the bows of the vessel, studying the volume of Shakespeare he had brought, learning favourite speeches. He must have plenty to recite if asked to display his talent. Common-sense warned him that, if taken on, he would not be given roles like Hamlet or King Lear. He would get tiny parts at first, perhaps two or three different ones in the same play. When that time came, he would have to memorise his lines fast – and faultlessly.

By the end of the voyage he had greatly enlarged his acquaintance with Shakespeare. His father would have been disappointed to see that he was no more attracted to a ship's officer's career than he had been before.

His first glimpse of land was the craggy granite cliffs of Cornwall. They changed next morning to the smoother-faced red heights that a deck-hand told him meant they were near the Devon coast. The land behind was fresh green or dark purple. 'Heather,' said the seaman. 'Grows wild over the hills.' As the day advanced other land, more distant, loomed to port. That was Wales, apparently, where many of the people spoke a language all their own. Even the English could make nothing of it.

The two coasts seemed to thrust forward or sweep back with capes or bays, but as the hours passed they gradually closed in to form a channel. There was little sameness in the scenery, no monotony. Dan began to read less and look more. Finally he closed his book and studied the changing scene.

At times they were near enough to the English shore to see farms and churches and villages clustered round a small harbour. There were figures working in the fields, waggons and coaches moving along the roads. Once a gentleman reined in his horse to admire the graceful schooner passing by. Dan waved a good-natured greeting. The rider swept off his three-cornered hat to return the compliment. My first

Englishman! Dan thought. Was it a good omen – a welcome, even?

The land closed in on both sides. This must be a river-mouth. They passed two islands. 'Steep Holme and Flat Holme,' said the first mate, strolling by. No need to ask which was which. The first rose straight from the water in sheer green cliffs like a gigantic bun. The second was a positive pancake. 'Sign that we're getting near Bristol,' said the mate. Within a little while they were moored in the river on which the city stood.

It seemed late in the day to call on Mr Widdowson. Dan conquered his impatience and waited till next morning before seeking out the agent's office in a sidestreet just off the harbour. He handed his letter of introduction to the clerk who was standing at a high desk, copying correspondence into a book.

'What name shall I say, sir? Oh, Mr *Carnaby*?' There was a noticeable change of tone. Dan was soon ushered into the inner room.

A small pot-bellied man with ruddy cheeks jumped up to greet him, the letter in his hand. The other hand, with a majestic sweeping gesture, held out an open snuffbox, then hastily withdrew it with a murmur of apology.

'Your pardon, Mr Carnaby! You will not

have developed this deplorable habit?'

'No, sir.'

'Quite so. At your age.'

But I must practise that gesture, Dan told himself. It might be called for in some part he would have to play. Like bowing or doffing his hat, he must be able to do it with an air, not as if it were for the first time. He would need to learn how to take snuff, too, or at least appear to.

Mr Widdowson waved him to a chair, made respectful inquiries about his father, and then resumed his own seat. He studied the letter in front of him.

'I will, of course, give you any assistance I can.'

'That is most kind of you—'

'But the playhouse, I must confess, is not a field with which I am familiar. A strange choice, if I may say so, for a lad of family like yours – and with such remarkable opportunities.' Mr Widdowson sounded puzzled and cautiously disapproving. 'Your father's connections! The respected name of Carnaby—'

'I have four brothers, sir. We do not all want to do the same. And I have my father's permission.'

'Of course, of course. And if I *can* help—'

'Is there a playhouse in Bristol?'

The agent hesitated. 'Er . . . yes – and no.' It

seemed unsure from season to season, he explained. There were constant difficulties. Managers came and went.

The present theatre had been opened only a few years ago. 1766, he thought. Thomas King had given up in 1771. 'Heavy gambling losses,' said Mr Widdowson with disapproval. James Dodd had taken over. 'He became involved in public scandal. So, *he* had to go. He has just been replaced by a Mr Reddish. Quite well-known in London, I understand – he comes from the famous Drury Lane theatre. They say he is trying to raise the standard. But . . . I don't know.'

It was easy to see why the agent did not know. When Dan asked if he often went to a play, he admitted that he had never set foot in the Bristol theatre.

Dan thought grimly, I am not going to get much help or encouragement here.

Otherwise this Widdowson seemed anxious enough to please – particularly, that is, to please Dan's father. Certainly he would make the desired arrangements with a bank to pay out Dan's modest allowance for the next six months. He would provide any practical advice or assistance the boy needed. And for a start he would insist on Dan's accepting his hospitality.

'We have a house in Queen Square, quite close,' he said, 'and plenty of room. My two sons, alas, have both left home, but we have daughters roughly your age. They will be delighted, I am sure . . .'

Perhaps, after all, things were looking up. Or were they?

Four

The Widdowsons had an imposing house. There was clearly money in being an agent. But Dan was not particularly interested in money.

Mrs Widdowson was, he quickly saw. Her home was more showy than his own, and the servants grander. She was effusive in her welcome. Would she have made such a fuss of *any* unknown young guest, arriving without warning?

Was it because he was a Carnaby? He had caught her husband's discreet whisper to her. That must be it. Dan was one of that Boston shipping family . . . important business connection . . . treat with care, even if he is only a lad.

His bedroom seemed vast after the tiny cabin on the schooner. Downstairs, in the superb drawing-room, he was presented to the two girls, flaxen Augusta and mousey Belinda, about a year younger. They were twittering as he entered. They had been hastily paraded by their mother.

They were . . . all right, he supposed. But he was really no judge.

They plied him with questions until dinner was

announced. They had the quaintest ideas of America, and were amazed that he had hardly ever set eyes on an Indian. He did not tell them that he had dressed up as one for the Boston Tea Party. The Widdowsons might disapprove.

Dinner was a treat after the ship's fare. He did justice to it.

Mrs Widdowson was concerned about his coming to England. What had his mother thought of this extraordinary playhouse notion? And his father – a gentleman in *his* position, so eminent in the world of shipping? Able to offer a splendid future to even the youngest of his sons?

'But there are other kinds of future, Mrs Widdowson,' said Dan. 'They want me to be happy. Try any kind of livelihood I like, so long as it's honest.'

'*Honest!*' The lady positively snorted. The idea of dishonesty could not arise with families of their class. ' "Suitable" would be a better word.'

Her husband came to Dan's rescue. 'I think, my dear, Mr Carnaby may think it a good idea to get his son out of Boston for a while. See a little of the world. There is some unrest there just now, a spirit of revolt. I am sure, of course' – Mr Widdowson coughed discreetly – 'a boy like Daniel would never get mixed up—'

'Of *course*! I should think not!'

'What's happening there?' asked the meek Belinda.

'Nothing to concern you, miss!' rapped out her mother.

But the subject had come up and must be explained. Mr Widdowson chose his words with care lest Dan quote him in a letter and give his father cause for offence.

'There is some public disorder, my dear. Though most of the people – like Daniel's own family – came from England many years ago, they don't see why they should still be ruled by our king and pay him taxes. This feeling seems specially strong in Boston.'

'It is, sir,' Dan admitted.

'They don't realise that they still depend on England for protection – against the French.'

'Not for some years now, sir, since General Wolfe took Quebec and they were driven out of Canada—'

'Well, perhaps not.' The agent sounded slightly nettled. 'But you still have to reckon with the Indians.'

'People think we can defend ourselves. If we have to fight Indians, we can do it better than redcoats shipped over from England.' Surely that made sense? The regular soldiers made easy targets as they marched along in columns beating their drums.

'Perhaps so, Daniel. But we need not argue that point. I am sure the Boston people do not mean to be disloyal. Everything will be settled. The link between the colonies and England is too valuable to both sides.'

Dan thought it was, too. So, he knew, did his father. Anyhow, his journey to England was purely his own idea, born of those evenings in New York. It was no scheme to keep him out of trouble at home.

No one seemed anxious to argue about politics. The girls were round-eyed at his plan to become an actor. Their mother's lips were pursed in disapproval when not pouring out indignant comments.

She had no more visited the Bristol theatre than her husband had. As for allowing her daughters to! It was no fit place for a well-brought-up female. 'I would not presume to criticise your parents,' she added hastily. 'It is, perhaps, different for boys.'

He wondered why. Were boys too stupid to understand the wicked things they heard in the playhouse? Or already so wicked by nature that nothing would make them any worse? He knew that many people at home disapproved – that was why, so far, there was no theatre in Boston – but he had imagined the English were more relaxed. Not all of them, it seemed.

Clearly there would be no happy theatre visit with the Widdowsons. He would have to go alone. He made respectful apologies to his hostess and asked leave to visit the theatre tomorrow evening. 'Of course,' she said grandly between gritted teeth. 'It is what you have come to England for. So if your parents approve . . .'

Augusta and Belinda remained silent. They looked pious and disapproving – and disappointed.

The Bristol theatre was in King Street, not far away. He learnt from a playbill next morning that the piece would be *The Conscious Lovers*, which he had never heard of, at six o'clock.

He had not been warned that only the most expensive seats, in the boxes, could be reserved. To make sure of a seat you had to buy your ticket in advance and send a servant to occupy your place until you arrived. The doors opened for this purpose as early as four o'clock.

It was after five when he arrived at the pit entrance in its courtyard, bought his ticket, followed an underground passage, and found the auditorium packed solid with chattering humanity.

It looked hopeless for a few moments. Fortunately there were no separate seats, only backless benches, and a burly footman had sprawled himself over-generously in the second row. He good-naturedly made space for Dan.

It looked quite an elegant playhouse, decorated in green and gold. Dan raised his eyes. There were still the empty boxes to left and right of the stage. Above the pit were two circles, and above them a gallery, the cheapest seating of all, used by the humblest classes. When the burly footman's master arrived to take his seat, the servant retired respectfully to watch the play from above. The whole theatre held about a thousand.

Within half an hour the crowd around Dan had changed almost completely as the real audience arrived and their seat-holders bowed and slipped away. Looking up again he saw grand people arranging themselves in the boxes, ladies with masses of shining hair, dotted with jewels, gracefully wielding fans. Their fine gentlemen were for once taking a back seat.

There were clearly plenty of people in Bristol who did not share Mrs Widdowson's attitude to the theatre.

The musicians struck up. The curtain rose.

28

Scores of candles danced brilliantly above, spiked on metal circles suspended over the stage, lighting up the painted canvas scenery. Now, at last, the actors and actresses came sweeping forward to meet the roar of welcoming applause.

Dan forgot the audience. He surrendered to the spell he had first fallen under in New York.

The Conscious Lovers had not the same magic as Shakespeare's plays. It was in prose not poetry, but the prose gave it a powerful reality of its own. It had been written by a man named Steele about fifty years ago.

It was good to see this sort of comedy. If he won his chance to get on the stage he would need to master all these different styles. Prose sounded easy, but it might prove harder. The regular rhythm of verse helped you to remember.

As scene followed scene, Dan tried to imagine which of the parts he might conceivably be given to play. One of the young men, most likely. Bevil, whose father wanted him to marry Lucinda but who himself wanted to marry a foreign girl he had met abroad? Or the other young man, Bevil's friend, who was really in love with Lucinda and would marry her if only the switch could be worked? There was a splendid scene when, through a misunderstanding, Bevil's friend challenged him to a duel. A duel, Dan quickly learnt, was always good business in the theatre. Whether with pistols or rapiers.

Don't be a conceited fool, he told himself sharply. Who is going to offer you a part like either of those? You may spend ages as a serving man with about two lines to say. Yes, sir. Certainly, madam.

Never mind. However long it took, he was determined.

The play ended. The conscious lovers paired off in the way they wished. One of the actresses recited an epilogue in rhymed couplets. More applause. Then out into the summer night. Carriages. Ladies carried off in ornamental chairs, borne by servants fore and aft. Gentlemen walking away in chattering groups.

Dan made for Queen Square, happy in his own dreams.

Tomorrow morning he would go back to King Street, beg to see the manager, plead for a chance.

If he got it he would have to thank the Widdowsons for their hospitality and find suitable lodgings elsewhere. He could not possibly trouble them further. He would have long working hours, performances and rehearsals and learning his lines, which would not combine with their mealtimes. It was most generous of them. He would write and tell his father how wonderful they had been . . .

This was a bit of acting which, if he got the chance, he would perform with zest.

Five

'I'm afraid you'll be unlucky,' said the man on the door. 'He's a very busy gentleman, Mr Reddish. Things crop up. Always do in this theatre game.'

'I can quite understand,' said Dan politely. Noises came from within. Angry men, weeping women: rehearsals of the next play, he guessed. Loud hammering, the screech of a saw: carpenters making new scenery.

'I'll see what I can do for you.' The old doorman limped away. Dan waited, deep in prayer.

The man came back. 'You're in luck, young man. He'll spare you a minute.'

'Oh, thank you!'

Remembering what his father would have done, Dan showed his appreciation. He dropped a coin into the hand conveniently held out for it.

Samuel Reddish swept in, a long roll of script curling from his fingers. He had an air. Dan knew that he was a well-known actor in London and had been brought down to King Street to pull things together.

'Now?' he demanded.

Dan had prepared a little speech and plunged into it.

'And where do you come from?'

'Boston, sir.'

'Ah, Lincolnshire. A fine town. One of the finest in England.'

'No, sir. In Massachusetts. The colonies.'

'The *colonies*? A long way, indeed!'

'But worth it, sir. For a play like last night's.'

This was the obvious cue to pour out his enthusiasm and the ambition that had brought him across the Atlantic. Mr Reddish lapped up his admiration and agreed. If Americans wanted to act they could not do better than learn their trade in England.

'And then in time to start theatres of their own?'

Mr Reddish seemed to wane in his enthusiasm. Starting a theatre was not so simple. He could clearly see a time when English actors might not find summer tours in the colonies for work during the closed season at home.

The conversation was interrupted by a tap on the door and the entry of the old door-man. He murmured something apologetically in the manager's ear. Mr Reddish sprang up almost eagerly.

'I am sorry, young man. Something urgent I must attend to. I fear there is nothing at this moment I can offer you. I can only wish you luck.'

Dan bowed and withdrew. He guessed that this scene was often repeated. The doorman had entered promptly on cue.

At dinner even Mrs Widdowson showed sympathy. 'I realise it was something you badly wanted. Will you give up now, and go home?'

'Oh, no.' Dan kept his voice bland. 'I never expected anything at the first attempt.'

Her husband's regret sounded more real. 'You caught Mr Reddish on a bad day. He had an unfortunate experience last night. Taking the air – walking along the road to Durdham Down – he was stopped by three scoundrels and robbed of nine guineas. It was the talk of the town this morning.'

Dan made a face. 'I certainly chose a bad moment.'

'And there was something else, probably much more serious. The theatre heard yesterday, they're not going to get their royal patent.'

'What does that mean, sir?'

'I had to ask round myself. Luckily, in a coffee house, there is always someone who knows all about everything. I thought it might affect you, so I'd better pick up what I could.'

'That was kind of you, sir.'

'Long ago, a law was passed saying you could only open a playhouse with the King's permission – what they call a royal patent. That's why they speak of the Theatre Royal, Drury Lane. There's only one other, in Covent Garden. Two others open only in the summer when the royal ones are closed.'

'What about places like Bristol?'

'Strictly, they're breaking the law. The magistrates could close them down and fine the people running them. But they might make themselves very unpopular, so they seldom interfere. The actors take their chance. Dozens of towns in England have theatres now. But they'd feel safer if they had a royal patent– it's like a licence.'

Bath, barely a dozen miles away, had got one just a few years ago. Its playhouse had officially become the 'Theatre Royal' in 1768, like those in London. Soon there was another, in Norwich, and now about ten towns were striving for the distinction. Bristol was still trying. People argued that, being a much bigger city than Bath, it had a better right to the honour. But yesterday the news had come that once more their plea had got them nowhere. No wonder Mr Reddish had been in a black mood.

At bedtime, as the young people gathered at the foot of the stairs to collect their lighted candles, Augusta's free hand plucked at Dan's sleeve.

'You won't go back to Boston yet?' she whispered.

He shook his head. 'Not likely.'

'What will you do?'

'I think Bath would be a good idea.'

He would be on his own now. He had made a mess of that vital interview with Mr Reddish. If he was given an interview in Bath, he must not make a mess of it again.

He would be on his own in another sense. It might be good to escape from the tiresome Mrs Widdowson and her insipid daughters, but their hospitality had been welcome enough. From tomorrow he would have to pay for every bite and sup – and for a roof over his head at night.

Luckily his father had been generous. He was not going to have his son a beggar in a distant land. Mr Widdowson had made arrangements and explained how he could draw his allowance wherever he found himself. But the money would not last forever. Before it gave out, Dan vowed, he must find work and some sort of wage. He would not go back to Boston with his tail between his legs.

It was a pleasant two-hour drive next morning. His high outside seat on the coach gave him splendid views of the rolling green hills and snippety curves of blue river flowing down from Bath. His spirits rose. The real adventure was about to begin. Dan Carnaby, alone against the world!

Bath itself was an odd name for a town. It came from its hot mineral springs which people came to drink and bathe in. The ancient Romans had done. People still did. Either way, it was good for your health.

He wondered if the city would *look* ancient Roman, like the engravings he had seen of the Colosseum and long, arched aqueducts such as the Pont du Gard in France. But Bath, now it came in sight, was a surprise – and at first a disappointment.

Not a Roman ruin to be seen. Quite the oldest building was a massive church, an abbey, dating from the time of the monks. You could see most of the city in one sweeping glance. It was packed into the bottom of a deep valley but nowadays was beginning to climb the surrounding hillsides. It all seemed to be built of the same biscuit-coloured stone.

This is not *ancient*, he told himself. Most of it might have been built yesterday. In several directions he could make out gangs of workmen, like ants, swarming on half-finished sites. Bath might have been any rapidly developing area in a New England colony. But it was clearly not a place where men bought land and built homes exactly as they fancied. The houses matched, they joined each other in long lines, often curved, dignified and symmetrical. Being built of the same coloured stone emphasised the artistic effect.

Mrs Widdowson had recommended the Pelican as a respectable inn for a young gentleman travelling alone: 'Your father would approve.' Dan accepted her advice, at least for tonight. It would probably be expensive but it would be pointless to start searching for cheap lodgings until he was sure of at least some temporary work. He might be taking the road for some other town.

The Pelican was just upstream from a fine new bridge that was being built across the Avon. He paused to look at its unusual design. It was going to be lined with houses on both sides. 'Shops, actually,' a man told him, noting his interest, 'like the famous old bridge in Florence.' You could learn a lot in this town, Dan told himself.

The Pelican had a spacious courtyard and colourful gardens stretching down to the river. There was an inexpensive single room available. He was disappointed to learn that there was no play at the theatre that night. Despite all the visitors attracted to Bath, there were not enough to provide an audience six days a week.

He had a problem now. He had meant to do as he had done at Bristol: begin by seeing a play and ask for an interview the following day, when he had a clearer idea of what the place and people were like. They might be more sympathetic if he was able to make sensible comments on the performance and express his admiration, provided that it was sincere.

In the end, however, his impatience overcame him. It might be foolish, but he could not wait two days to see if his luck had changed. So, after a cup of coffee and some bread and cheese, he set off to find the theatre.

It was close to the abbey, in a byway called Orchard Street, because the monks had grown their apples there. To his relief the door was ajar. The man behind it had a friendly smile.

'It would be the *young* Mr Palmer you'd have to see. Mr Palmer senior has practically handed things over to him now. He travels all over, young Mr Palmer does, hunting for talent. He should be in Worcester at this moment—'

Dan felt a stab of alarm. When would this man be back? Had his luck changed? Or did it just mean more suspense before he had to face the fact that it had not?

'But you're in luck today, as it happens,' the man went on. 'His plans have altered. He's not leaving till tomorrow. What name shall I say, sir?'

Five minutes later, Dan had poured out his story. Palmer was sympathetic, but shrewd . . . He assessed Dan with half-closed eyes. 'Can you give me a sample?'

'Yes, sir. Shakespeare, sir?'

'Excellent.'

'*Twelfth Night*, sir. Malvolio.' Dan launched into a favourite passage he had known by heart for years.

'Yes,' said Palmer, 'though if we were playing *Twelfth Night* this season I fear we could not offer you a leading part like that. Sebastian, now—'

'Viola's twin brother?' Dan's quick response seemed to make a good impression.

'That's how I could see you. You look the age.

You look right in other ways. So many plays have a part for a good-looking youth to pair off with a beautiful girl. Even if there isn't, you can always *use* him – as a page or a young singer—'

'I *can* sing, a little, sir,' said Dan modestly. But it was not a moment to be too modest. 'Or I could dress older, if need be.'

'It so happens I am watching out for somebody. It's not the main object of my mission, but . . .' Palmer hesitated. 'If I could tick *that* off my little list, my mind would be freer for more important problems. Suppose I offered you a trial?'

'Oh, would you, sir?'

'A pound a week, to start with.'

'Thank you, sir!'

Palmer stood up. 'In four days we shall be reviving *The Merchant of Venice*. You would look well as Lorenzo.'

'Bassanio's friend? Who runs off with Shylock's daughter?'

'You know the play. Good. Report for the first rehearsal at nine tomorrow morning. Try to be word-perfect. You'll need a script.'

'I have a book of Shakespeare's plays, sir—'

'But you can't possibly know what we're leaving out!'

Palmer rummaged in a desk and tossed him a

soiled and slightly tattered roll of manuscript. 'That's all *you'll* need.'

Dan bowed himself out. His head was in a whirl of glory.

Six

For the rest of the afternoon he had planned to explore the city. Now he had no time to kill. He must be word-perfect by nine o'clock tomorrow. It was possible. Just.

The riverside gardens of the Pelican were secluded, fresh and beautiful. He found a private corner and stayed there almost until twilight. The script had been well-used by predecessors in the part. They had pencilled in changes and cuts and stage directions which for the moment baffled him. '*L2E*'? That proved to mean 'left, second entrance', indicating between which two wings of flat scenery he should come onstage.

The script carried only Lorenzo's lines and the cues with which other characters ended or began. If he had not read the play before, he would have had no notion of what happened or was said between his own contributions. It was doubly lucky he had his printed copy of the whole play. He could refresh his memory of the characters, what they were like, and what they had just said that his own lines were alluding to.

I must seem to know what I'm talking about as well, he told himself.

Next morning he was punctual at the door in Orchard Street before the clocks began to strike. Within a few minutes, quite a cluster of men and women were gathered behind the sloping stage. The curtain was up. In the twilit gloom overhead he could make out the hanging chandeliers, with their hoops of unlit candles and a positive web of ropes. It looked a tangle, but he soon learnt what an efficient system it was for changing the scenery.

'You're to report to Mr Henderson,' the door-keeper said, pointing out a fair-haired, youngish man of solid build. 'Mr Palmer left him a note to explain.'

Dan had heard about John Henderson from a servant at the inn. He was only in his mid-twenties and had come down from London a year or two ago with a recommendation from the great David Garrick. People had not thought much of him at first – he came of very poor family and was not impressive to look at – but he had soon surprised them. By the time he had played Hamlet, Richard III and Hotspur, he had proved his quality. In his first season he had taken thirty different parts. He was a demon for work. He had started on a guinea a week (only a shilling

44

more than me, thought Dan). It was a humbling thought. Could he prove himself of equal value to the company?

He walked across and modestly presented himself. Henderson welcomed him pleasantly. 'Ah, our new Lorenzo? Mr Palmer thought you should have a trial. You have come so far. America! Well, we shall see.'

He was not strikingly handsome, he put on no airs, but there was a determination in his face. Dan took to him. He was lucky to be working under this man. He must justify the opportunity.

As he answered Henderson's questions, the throng thickened. In the distance, just visible among the shifting heads and shoulders, he noticed a boy no older than himself. Not quite so tall, even, but – he had to admit with a pang of faint alarm – much better looking.

Had he a rival?

The boy turned and came in their direction. How elegant he looked in that trim tail-coat and those white skin-tight breeches! And goodness, his features – those parted lips, that delicate but determined little chin above the frothy lace of the cravat at his throat. For any one who liked that 'pretty boy' type—

Dan did not. He felt a surge of resentment, followed by an instant backwash of relief. As Henderson said, 'Ah, Jessica, allow me to present our new Lorenzo,' that relief strengthened to positive delight. Henderson spoilt that by adding formally, 'Mrs Stone – Mr Daniel Carnaby. Mr Carnaby – Mrs Stone.' Then an urgent shout from the auditorium sent him hurrying away.

Mrs? Was it possible? All too possible. She looked no older than himself. But girls married earlier than boys; especially girls like this one. Politely he asked, 'Is your husband in the company?'

She stared. 'Goodness! I *have* no husband.'

'But Mr Henderson said "Mrs Stone"—'

'Every actress is "Mrs" on the playbill. It's a sign that she's respectable . . . even if sometimes she isn't. It would be an insult to leave it out.'

'So, I call you "Mrs Stone"?'

'Only on public occasions.' She had a friendly smile. 'We shall be working together. You may call me "Jessica". It is *really* my first name, not just in the play. It's rather unusual, isn't it? My parents took it from Shakespeare.'

'I like it.'

'I should explain,' she said, 'just to reassure you: this is not *meant* to be a dress-rehearsal.' She indicated the tight-fitting breeches. 'I put these on to practise the elopement scene – that jump off the balcony. Mr Henderson is emphatic we must get it right, especially as you're new. I need to see where my feet are landing, and so do you if you're going to catch me cleanly. You won't want me coming over that balcony in a flurry of skirts and petticoats . . .'

'Indeed no.' Dan put on his most proper expression. He must not stare at those legs. You saw nothing like that in Boston. Shakespeare, of course, had had no actresses, so the first Jessica would have been a boy pretending to be a girl pretending (for her escape) to be a boy. He would have worn the doublet and hose of those days. Almost two centuries later, with plays presented mostly in the costumes of their own 1770s, this Jessica had stockings and breeches much like his own, though his were of a more elegant cut.

'So,' she said, 'as we're not needed for the moment, shall we study the situation?'

They walked upstage to the piece of scenery concerned. The flat wing of wood and canvas was already standing in its groove. Its high balconied window was often used for a romantic escape route or means of unlawful entry.

It was not absolutely essential for Jessica to make her jump. She had a line, 'Here catch this casket – it is worth the pains—' and Dan had to bid her 'descend', but she could have come downstairs to street-level and used the door. In the theatre, though, Dan quickly learnt, you must extract all possible entertainment for the public. If you had a girl in the company with legs like Jessica's, clad as Shakespeare indicated 'in the lovely garnish of a boy', it was a good idea to let her jump and show them. It was such skills Dan must learn in his chosen career.

The wall of Shylock's house might only be painted cloth, but the projecting balcony was stoutly built. 'It's nothing,' Jessica assured him. 'I could stand on the parapet and jump.'

'Rather high for that,' he said anxiously. 'Why not just sit on it – and drop?'

'Not dramatic enough! Never waste an opportunity.'

'Certainly not.' Henderson had rejoined them. 'It's not the actual height that matters, it's the illusion.' They considered various possibilities. 'This will be best,' he said at last.

'It's not very dignified,' she objected. It meant scrambling over the balcony, turning her back on the audience, and dangling at arm's length before dropping into Lorenzo's upstretched arms.

'We must see it as the audience will,' said Henderson.

Dan could, and at closer quarters. Jessica obviously could not. 'Very well, Mr Henderson,' she said.

'Try it.' They did, and he seemed satisfied. 'You make a very effective contrast. Your fair hair, Mr Carnaby's almost black – gold and ebony! And *you* have such fine, delicate features—' He stopped, finding it hard to finish.

'I'm sorry about my big nose,' said Dan helpfully.

'What's wrong with it?' demanded the girl rushing to the rescue. 'It's not big. I'd call it commanding. The right nose for a man!'

'I'll leave you to argue it out,' said Henderson, turning away.

'We must get this perfect,' Dan said. 'We don't want any accidents.'

They rehearsed in low voices, not to disturb the others downstage. She slipped over the balcony gracefully, and dangled for a few moments, those elegant legs outspread against the painted canvas wall. He stood ready to catch her. Oddly, he had a sudden flash of memory – of a much-loved pony he had possessed as a child. He had an impulse . . .

She let go. She dropped, feather-light, precisely as she was meant to, into his waiting arms. She spoke her next line, to greet the entrance of Lorenzo's friend Salarino: 'What, art thou come?' As Salarino was obviously not there, they spoke the last few lines to their own exit. Then, in her everyday voice, she remarked casually, 'I imagine you are fond of cats?' She gave him an odd, amused look.

'Cats?' he echoed, puzzled. 'No, dogs more. And horses—'

Then he realised, and felt the hot blood rush to his face. That almost irresistible impulse a minute ago, could it be that he had *not* resisted it? His hands had been upstretched. Had he touched her, as he would have touched that pony long ago?

Thank God, she did not look mortally offended. 'Anyhow,' she said lightly, 'I am no cat. Though I think I could scratch – if I had to. It's strange, you know. You can refer to a man as a "gay young dog" and he does not mind. He takes it as a compliment.'

Henderson was calling from the front. Playing Shylock himself, he wanted to go through a scene with his 'daughter'.

Dan almost mopped his brow. He hoped he

had not offended this divine young creature. He must obviously beware of the least familiarity, however accidental. Mustn't put a foot wrong, he told himself sternly. Much less a hand!

She seemed to have forgiven him. When he encountered her again she was all smiles. 'Cheer up,' she whispered. 'Mr Henderson thinks you'll do. He asked how we'd got on.'

She must have given a favourable account of him.

After the long rehearsal, she asked if he had found good lodgings. Where was he?

'I was at the Pelican last night. I can't afford to go on there. Much too expensive.'

'The door-keeper will advise you.'

'Are you in a lodging house?' He must sound casual.

'Oh, yes. On Abbey Green. Very close. It's called that because the monks played bowls there in the old days.'

All this part of Bath had once been part of the monastery. Now little remained but the abbey church.

'I'm afraid we're full up there.' Jessica seemed genuinely sorry. 'Anyhow, some landladies don't favour ladies and gentlemen in the same house, unless they're husband and wife, of course. With stage people they're very careful of their reputation.'

'I shall find somewhere,' he said.

When the door-keeper reeled off several addresses, he pounced on another house in Abbey Green and later discovered he was only two doors away from Jessica's lodging. But he saw little of her, outside the theatre, in those first few days.

His own lodging was a humbler one. His landlady, Mrs Askew, was kindly; to himself rather motherly in view of his age. She stood no nonsense from his two fellow-lodgers, little Bradley and lanky Ruddock, a partnership of old rascals who specialised in clown parts. Ruddock was Irish and talked wistfully of his beloved Smock Alley Theatre, the Drury Lane of Dublin. England, he swore, would have been nowhere without Irish talent. Dan certainly found that half the people he'd heard of in the playhouse came from that other island.

Mrs Askew put on a good dinner before the evening performances, and a simple but substantial bedtime snack. Dan found this a lifesaver when he began to act himself, and for the first few weeks was almost too nervous to eat beforehand. Bradley and Ruddock preferred to take their final snack in the livelier atmosphere of a tavern. Their capacity for drink seemed inexhaustible.

He seldom had much in common with old men like them. The age gap was too great, and the difference in tastes and habits. But the theatre was a bond. He loved their endless stories, often scandalous and improper, about places where they had acted. They filled in the gaps in his own knowledge. Ruddock had even gone on one of the American tours. Naturally he had never seen Boston. He could not understand why Dan knew so little about Philadelphia and Williamsburg.

'They're all in different colonies,' Dan explained. 'Pennsylvania, Virginia, and so on. Our links are more with London. Because of the government.'

The old man was completely vague about that.

Bradley was helpful with practical information. Dan had not only to master his lines but the peculiar jargon of the stage, so that he could instantly understand a shouted instruction from Henderson. Bradley saved him the humiliation of having to ask.

'Right' and 'Left' were as you faced the audience. The 'prompt side' was always on the left and the scribbled letters on your script, 'OP' meant 'opposite prompt'. The prompter's copy was the 'book'. 'Up' and 'down' because the stage sloped up towards the back to give the audience a better view.

'The one unforgivable thing', Bradley warned him, 'is to force a principal character to turn his back on the audience. You're "upstaging" them – they must always face the audience. If you do that to some actresses, it's all hell let loose.'

Actors needed to carry an invisible chart of the stage area in their heads. Three bands running from side to side, each divided again into three, so that you had 'up left centre' or 'down right', or whatever precise indication Henderson gave you of where he wanted you to stand.

As bad as the captain's chart on a schooner, thought Dan, but you have to carry it all in your head.

Ruddock made occasional contributions. 'Do you know what we mean by a scissors cross?' he demanded. It was when two characters had to cross the stage at the same moment but in opposite directions. You had to watch out so that you did not collide.

'Risky way of life ours,' said Bradley. 'Never

know what will go wrong next. Plays fail, even theatres fail, you're out on the streets. Always some danger waiting in the wings!'

'*I am learning a great deal*,' wrote Dan in his first triumphant letter to his parents, reporting his success in finding work, '*but that is just what I have come for.*' He did not say too much about the two fellow-lodgers and concentrated rather on the motherly Mrs Askew. Jessica he did not mention at all. There was nothing really to say, he told himself defensively.

He dispatched this letter through the Widdowsons, to whom he wrote a shorter, but sincere, thankyou for their hospitality. It had been agreed that it would be best, for the time being, if his mail from home passed through the shipping office.

The short time before his own first appearance on the stage was so full that there was little scope for impatience. There were rehearsals in the daytime. In the evenings he attended other plays, marvelling at the capacity of the players to switch from one piece to another on the same day. He was certainly going to need all his vitality until he got used to it. It was good, after the repetitions and idle spells of the daytime rehearsals, to relax in his free seat and watch Jessica, apparently fresh as a daisy, playing a pert maidservant or a dutiful daughter.

It was a pity that his elopement with her in *The Merchant* had not been developed more importantly in the plot. But, if it had been, he might never have got the part of Lorenzo. The purpose of Jessica's flight was mainly to show Shylock as a deserted and distracted parent. Dan saw that his own scenes with her had been severely pruned.

In the last act, though, they had their own little chance of glory. They would be alone in the moonlit avenue of Portia's house at Belmont, while all the main characters were in Venice, acting the great trial scene of Antonio's deliverance from the moneylender.

Their dialogue was pure poetry. They had alternate four-line speeches, each starting with the same phrase, 'In such a night—' Entirely artificial, but, as the girl insisted, absolutely exquisite.

'Almost like a song, really,' he said.

'You're right. A duet.'

That repeated phrase created the illusion. They decided that, different though their voices were, boy's and girl's, they could achieve in their delivery quite a strikingly musical effect. They worked at it in private. Henderson made no comment or criticism. What with playing Shylock himself, and being generally responsible for the whole production, he now only had time for general supervision.

The curtain rose on that final scene. The lighting had been splendidly contrived. Jessica, those trim white breeches long ago discarded, was in a slim cascading dress that was itself like moonlight. Dan had the opening lines:

'The moon shines bright. In such a night as this,

When the sweet wind did gently kiss the trees—'

There was utter silence as they went on, answering each other, speech by speech. The audience seemed spellbound. What a contrast, he thought later, to their noisy but delighted response to Jessica's descent from the balcony!

The silence held until, all too soon, Jessica had to break off as they heard Stephano's running footsteps patter from the wings, cue for Dan's own cry, 'Who comes so fast in silence of the night?'

Soon the stage was crowded with the triumphant return from Venice of the other characters. Dan and Jessica had had their moment.

It had not gone unnoticed. As they left the theatre, to walk the few yards to Abbey Green, John Palmer greeted them. He had returned from his talent-spotting trip in time to see the second half of the play.

'Ah! Mr – Carnaby, isn't it? I gambled on you, but I think it came off?'

Seven

I have passed the first test, Dan told himself triumphantly. But I mustn't relax, he added – then laughed at the absurdity of the idea. What chance had he to relax?

New parts had constantly to be learnt. No play could be done many nights in succession, with such a limited population. A new play had to be put on or an old one revived, which for him meant a new one. Ruddock and Bradley had their heads stuffed with the half-remembered lines of all the pieces they had played in. If cast in a different part, they still had a general familiarity which must be invaluable.

Even Jessica, young as she was, already had a lot of experience. He envied her.

Bath was lucky in having such a constant stream of visitors coming to take the waters. They kept the theatre going, which the townspeople alone might not have managed to do.

'Bums on benches,' said Bradley coarsely. 'That's what you need in this business.'

Not all Dan's parts gave him as much to learn

as Lorenzo. As Mr Palmer had warned him, he might sometimes be worked in only to sing a song or appear as a servant. He might have to be cast as two or three nameless nobodies in the same play, striving to establish that each *was* a different character – as if anyone cared! The only consolation was in having fewer lines and cues to master. A big part in every play would have been an impossible burden for a newcomer.

It was natural that, when he was lucky enough to get a fair-sized part, he was brought into contact again with Jessica. They were, after all, the two youngest members of the company. On some of the mild autumn days, if they were not called to a general rehearsal, they would meet and run over their lines in the public gardens. Neither of their landladies would have approved of their doing this together indoors.

It was a happy arrangement. Even when it was rather one-sided – when Dan was scarcely involved and he was mainly hearing *her* recite *her* lines – they were both pleased to continue it. 'It may some day be a great help to me,' Dan insisted. 'I'm learning about these plays. Who knows, the day may come when I get a part in one at short notice?' It was giving him the sort of background familiarity that he envied in old troupers like Ruddock and Bradley.

Jessica seemed grateful. It was a pleasanter way to learn her part than sitting alone in her lodging house. She insisted that, when they had time left over, she must repay him by showing him round the little city. In his first days he had no chance to explore it.

'Where are these famous baths?' he asked.

'You haven't seen them?'

They were only a stone's throw from their lodgings, but in the opposite direction from the theatre. He had no cause to pass them.

'You can't miss them,' she said. 'There are galleries built all round. They're open to the public.'

That sounded interesting. 'I'd like to see them,' he said. 'But – aren't there *ladies*?'

'Of course. First thing in the morning is the fashionable time. Until ten or eleven. That's when all the grand people are there. Then the chairmen carry them to their lodgings to dress and have coffee, and the baths are refilled with clean water. I'll show you tomorrow.'

Ladies! What on earth did they wear? He dared not ask.

Jessica seemed very matter-of-fact as she

promised to meet him at nine. They had a rehearsal at ten.

There were several different baths. Far the biggest was the King's Bath, joined to the smaller Queen's Bath. As she had promised, there were raised galleries built on arches, from which one could look down into the water.

'I hope you are not disappointed?' she said artlessly.

'Disappointed? Why should I be?' He floundered a little, trying to sound casual. He had noted that tell-tale hint of mischief in her voice.

'No doubt you were expecting a parade of elegance? All our well-to-do visitors, dressed in the height of fashion? The pump-room is the place for that. Where they *drink* the waters.'

He had certainly not been expecting what he now saw below him. The ladies were clad in voluminous gowns of yellow canvas with immense sleeves. As the hot water welled up under the canvas it completely hid the shape beneath. The gentlemen wore yellow canvas drawers and waistcoats. Moving around looked difficult, the hot springs bubbling up fiercely from below, and even the gentlemen sometimes looked grateful for a helping hand from the attendants. Often they would sit down on stone seats below the surface, and the water would come up to their chins. Once, to Dan and Jessica's amusement, a rather small lady called for a 'cushion' to keep her head above water. When the woman attendant brought it, they saw it was a slab of stone.

Dan was surprised so many of the ladies were young and attractive. 'Surely', he said, 'they don't have gout? Like these old gentlemen?'

'I shouldn't imagine so. I hope I shall never have *their* trouble.' Her tone was grave. He wondered if it was one of those female afflictions it was safest not to inquire about.

Jessica, however, seeing his puzzlement, went on to explain. 'Most of these young ones hope taking the waters will help them to have children. They say King Charles II brought his queen because she seemed barren. Bath didn't do *her* any good, so the next king was his brother James.'

'Well, you don't have to worry about things like that,' he said cheerfully. 'You're not even married yet.'

'No. But I probably will be one day. And then I shall want children, I'm sure. I'm in no hurry. I've got to think of my career first. Get thoroughly established. Children can make things awkward if you're on the stage. You find your figure is suddenly unsuitable for the part; especially if it's a breeches part, as mine so often is. And however carefully you calculate when the baby will arrive, *they* don't always come on cue.'

How lucky, he thought, that I'm a boy. No, a man. I must think of myself as a man now.

It had been an extraordinary conversation. He had never before talked about marriage and babies, least of all with a girl. Indeed, he hardly thought about them. Presumably he himself would marry one day, everyone seemed to. But it was something for the far-off future. Better be, he told himself firmly. He too must establish himself. As the girl had said, think of one's career first. Easy! When did he think of anything else?

All the same, he was pleased to know that there was no young man in the background. No one to object to her friendship with himself. He did not want any one to upset that.

They continued their explorations on other days. Their lodgings, like the theatre itself, were in the oldest quarter of the town. They could see fragments of the borough walls, dating back hundreds of years, and see how small it must have been. When the monastery had been closed down, its vacant space had been built over with houses – like Abbey Green and Orchard

Street – but now Bath was bursting at the seams.

'You must see the new Assembly Rooms,' said Jessica. 'The upper ones, they've only been opened a year or two.'

They were the theatre's main rivals. When there was a ball or other evening entertainment, it meant poor business in Orchard Street.

They had to climb a steep street lined with tall, dignified new houses. Gay Street looked anything but gay. That was the strange thing about Bath. It seemed full of streets with unsuitable names: Trim Street and Quiet Street and even Cheap Street. Gay, Jessica explained, was a London surgeon who had owned the land and now lived in one of the houses built on it.

At the top they came to the Circus, but there was nothing very lively about that either. The houses were built in a circle, their frontages in ancient classical styles. 'What a lot you know,' he said.

She explained, 'My father was a schoolmaster.'

Finding out more about this girl could be even more interesting than exploring Bath.

They admired the Assembly Rooms and then the Royal Crescent. They stood on the hillside and gazed down over the city. Other hills closed it in on every side. The river curled through it like a silver ribbon.

'I love hills,' she said softly.

As they walked down, she told him more about herself. She had been born in a small town in the Cotswold Hills not far away. Her father had died. Her mother had married again – this time to a rich farmer.

'Such a *dull* man,' she said viciously. She added, 'Of course, he doesn't approve of me.'

Dan could not imagine anyone who would not.

Her mother had been young enough to start a second family. Jessica had been an only child.

'When babies started arriving,' she said, 'I felt more and more out of place. But Mother seemed happy enough, thank God.' Her thanks sounded rather grudging. 'If I had been a heifer I am sure my stepfather would have packed me off to the next market, to get me out of the way. As he couldn't do that, I saved him the trouble. And here I am.'

'Thank God.'

Last year she had been lucky enough to catch Mr Palmer's eye on one of his talent-spotting journeys. She had seized her chance. Her youth and looks made her suitable for breeches parts so she had specialised in them.

'It was lucky,' she told Dan. 'So many actresses don't like them. They haven't the figure – or if they have, they don't fancy exposing it on the public stage—'

He grinned. 'But you're shameless?'

'Absolutely.' She grinned back.

He mentioned his new friend now in his letters home. But cautiously. He wanted to assure his mother that he was not lonely or unhappy in England. She must not get any wrong ideas though, so he did not say too much about Jessica. He did not mention her 'breeches parts' – who at home would even know the term? Some would think it indelicate.

'Are there *enough* parts like that?' he asked Jessica. He could think of several instances in Shakespeare. But surely you could not use the idea in play after play, a girl disguising herself as a man? It would get monotonous.

She reassured him. When anything was so popular with audiences the writers would find some excuse to work it in. George Farquhar, a young Irish writer dead long ago, had been particularly good and his plays were still popular. One, *The Recruiting Officer*, had a magistrate's daughter, Silvia, running away from home in male dress and then being sentenced by her own father, who did not recognise her, to be drafted into the army. Jessica had played the part and loved it.

Sometimes the character was meant to *be* a man but was played by an actress, like Sir Harry Wildair in another Farquhar comedy, *The Constant Couple*. 'And there was the famous Peg Woffington, you've heard of her? The first time she was in *The Beggar's Opera* she was Polly – but she ended with the leading part as Macheath, the highwayman! I'd like to do that some day.'

Some people imagined that a woman playing such roles must be mannish. 'Do you think *I* am mannish?'

'That thought would never occur to me!'

'Nell Gwyn was one of the first to play breeches parts. And we all know about *her* and Charles II! Peg Woffington had a love affair with David Garrick.'

The weeks passed. Months now. Autumn gave place to winter. Bath was bright in the evenings: every house carried an outside light to break the darkness.

Dan was tried out in longer parts, and was called in if someone fell sick. He was a quick study and was getting a reputation for being dependable.

He played Sir Andrew Aguecheek, the young fool in *Twelfth Night*, and enjoyed the chance of comedy. He played as foil to old Bradley, a natural Toby Belch, and had a hilarious scene with Jessica, playing the Duke's messenger, Cesario, challenging her to a duel, of which both of them were equally scared. He had the opportunity, too, of finding out how much good drama had been written since Shakespeare's day.

John Henderson – Shandy, as the senior members of the company were allowed to call him – was a demon for work, but a good-natured demon and just the sort of teacher Dan needed. Onstage, and behind it, Henderson was king. Palmer, who managed the business of the theatre for his father, was a very different, but equally dynamic, character.

The Palmers were a well-known family in the neighbourhood. Young Palmer had hankered after an army career but had not achieved it, and he had found an outlet for his energy in fox-hunting. When he was drawn into the business of Orchard Street, he had found that outlet in his constant travels by coach across the country, visiting other playhouses and recruiting fresh actors and actresses in whom he saw promise.

Coaches had a fascination for him. Dan heard

him declare that with proper organisation of the stagecoaches, passing constantly to and fro across the country, the delivery of letters could be made vastly quicker and more reliable. It was interesting, a few years later, to see his claim proved true. Before then, though, Palmer's enthusiasm for coaches landed Dan and Jessica in a rather alarming adventure.

Eight

Mr Widdowson's gloomy view of the prospects for the Bristol theatre had been correct. The gossip from that city was of constant disappointments. It seemed, now, there was no future for King Street.

It was John Palmer of Bath who saved the situation.

Dan heard the news after a morning rehearsal at Orchard Street. 'So, in future,' Palmer concluded his announcement, 'our two theatres will run in double harness. You will play in both cities, on alternate nights.'

They broke up amid a buzz of discussion.

Dan thought it a good idea. The Carnaby in him recognised it as a sound business proposition. Neither place had a big enough public to fill it six nights a week.

That was the money side. But also, playing only three nights in each city, they would not have to change their programme so often. That meant, for himself in particular, fewer new parts to memorise.

Not everybody was quite so pleased. Over their dinner that evening, Ruddock and Bradley were grumbling hard.

'We'll be flashing to and fro like a shuttle,' Bradley complained. 'How he thinks we can do it—'

For once, Dan broke in. 'Coaches,' he said.

'And the scenery?' said Ruddock. 'He can't pack the scenery into a coach.'

'That man's crazy about coaches,' said Bradley. 'We'll be out on the road till midnight.'

What really irked the pair was the loss of their late-night drinking on the three alternate evenings every week when they would be playing in Bristol and driving back afterwards.

As usual, the coach enthusiast solved the scenery problem. He had two special coaches built for the company.

'*We call them the caterpillars,*' Dan wrote to his family. '*They look so long. But the flats have to be long. When they are stood upright in their grooves they go out of sight. Of course you can roll the canvas, and joint some of the wooden sections, but there is a limit. The two caterpillars will take all of us, and the scenery and costumes and props.*'

How much this would interest his parents he did not know, but he was anxious to take their minds off the troubles they seemed to be having at their end.

The dispute with the London government had not been solved. Boston had been taking such a lead that the British put the whole blame on its tiresome citizens. The port was closed. Boston was deprived of its status as capital of Massachusetts. How, Dan wondered angrily, could that be done by a parliament sitting in London?

'*Closing the port,*' wrote his father, '*will make difficulties for business. I shall not be able to send letters to you by schooner. We shall find ways to get round these problems. I am sure Mr Widdowson will help. There are bound to be delays, though. It is as well that you are not planning your return home. Better to put that out of your mind for the present.*'

It had not been in Dan's mind. But from his own selfish point of view the news was welcome. There would be no pleading letters from his mother, asking how much longer he would have to stay in England.

He had just been given his best part so far, in Shakespeare's comedy, *Much Ado About Nothing*. Needless to say, Henderson was playing the lead: Benedick, the confirmed bachelor, who sparred all through the play with the quick-witted Beatrice he was to marry at the end. Jessica would have loved to play Beatrice, but of course it must go to the first lady in the company. In a year or two, she vowed, her time would come.

Anyhow, *Much Ado* was packed with good parts. There was a most villainous villain, John, bastard brother to the kindly Prince of Aragon; it was John who made all the trouble. There were two clownish officers of the watch, Dogberry and Verges – perfect for Bradley and Ruddock. And Jessica, who was nerving herself to be only one of the attendant gentlewomen, Ursula or Margaret, was delighted to find herself Beatrice's beautiful cousin Hero.

'What an odd name for a girl!' Dan said. She assured him it was all right. There was a famous female Hero in Greek legend.

'And I have to marry *you* at the end,' she cried in mock-disgust. He knew that really she was as pleased as he was that he had been given such an important part.

Count Claudio, Benedick's friend, was a young lord of Florence. It was all arranged that he should marry Hero (another thing that Dan found gratifying), but of course the villain had been busy, determined to wreck everything, spreading a false story that she was having an affair with another man. Dan was the central figure in the most dramatic scene he had yet been given to play. He had to stand waiting at the altar for his bride and, when she appeared, reject her with a burst of fury and the scornful cry to her father, 'Give not this rotten orange to your friend!'

That line became a secret joke between Jessica and himself. 'And how is the rotten orange?' he would ask her each morning when they met. The comedy, of course, had a happy ending, when the music struck up and they joined hands in the dance.

It was at the Bristol performance, when they lined up to make their final bows, that he saw the Widdowsons.

So they had come. Not only come but, as they had a position to keep up in the city, they had taken an expensive box . . .

. . . And apparently enjoyed the play. Mrs Widdowson was beaming. The girls had jumped up and were clapping excitedly. He could only cast a smile in their direction and hope they would read it as a personal response.

Would they come round afterwards? They did not. Not being regular play-goers, they would not realise it was allowed. Perhaps in a day or two Mr Widdowson would write a polite little message.

He did, but it was not just polite – it was warm. They all hoped to see him again in other plays. It was the first such letter Dan had ever received from anyone. It was not to be the last.

Backstage, the workmen were feverishly dismantling the scenery and carrying it out to the coaches. The men, Bradley and Ruddock especially, were drinking fast so that they would not become too thirsty as they travelled the twelve miles to Bath. Few people, even among the ladies, were troubling to change completely out of the costumes they had worn in the last scene. They were keen not to delay the departure.

The first caterpillar got away. Jessica and the other ladies came out and took the seats kept for them. He knew that sufficient space would be left beside her before the door was slammed. Unless her role demanded it, she avoided the wide hooped skirts and long stiff stays of fashion. She preferred free-flowing dresses, narrowing to a high trim waist. So there was room for a slim young man as well, though it was rather a tight fit. Neither of them minded that.

The driver checked that they were all aboard and mounted his box. They wheeled out into the moonlit street and were off.

For a time the noisy chatter continued. Congratulations, complaints (about the Bristol staff), impressions of the evening's success, flew to and fro. 'You were magnificent,' Dan whispered. 'So were you,' she answered. 'Quite an eye-opener – even to *our* people.'

But it had been a long day. The gossip slackened. Eyes closed. Then, with startling suddenness, the coach stopped. Those who had been dozing fell against each other and woke with stammered apologies. Outside, a voice rang clear.

'Keep your hands up, coachman! Hang on to your reins; keep your team steady. If you reach for your gun, I'll blow your brains out!'

'It's a highwayman!' gasped one of the ladies.

'It'll be that dreadful Morgan!' said another.

Dan knew the name. It was a Welshman who worked the roads of the West Country. He might not be fearless but he was certainly ruthless. He had only to be caught once and it would mean the gallows. So he was merciless to anyone who resisted. For the same reason, folks said, he preferred to work alone. An accomplice might one day be bribed to give him away.

'Listen, all of you, you in the coach,' the voice went on. 'I have your driver covered. So don't try anything. If you do – any of you – I'll blow *his* brains out. You wouldn't want that now, any of you? So listen. Ladies first. One at a time. Hold up your jewels – in the moonlight, so's I can see 'em. Then put 'em in the bag. I've thrown it down at the side o' the road. Be good now, an' no harm'll come.'

'Oh, my poor necklace,' Jessica whispered in distress. Dan knew that necklace. It was of no great value. She had been given it in childhood. By her father, just before he died. For that reason it was beyond price.

A wild anger swept through him. He thought rapidly. This Morgan always worked alone. He must be in front of the coach, where he could cover the driver on his box. He must be slightly to the right-hand side – Dan could tell from the direction of his voice. Morgan must be able to see each lady as she got out to surrender her valuables.

So this left side of the coach was outside the Welshman's vision. He must take a chance that no armed passenger would slip out silently and, risking his life or that of the unfortunate coachman, creep forward and attack. Presumably

Morgan's experience to date had shown that passengers never did get out and assail him. They left that sort of thing to the drivers, who usually had guards to help them.

There was one snag from Dan's point of view. He felt pretty certain that no one in the company had a loaded pistol. The thing bulging in his own pocket was a harmless stage property. It was not in Shakespeare. It had been introduced to heighten the tension when there was talk of Benedick challenging Claudio to a duel.

With luck, though – and how much luck Dan was going to need! – the sight of it would distract this Morgan. Just long enough for the driver to grab the loaded blunderbuss under his seat. It was a desperate gamble. But he had only a few moments to make up his mind. If he had longer, he might have seen that it was possible suicide.

Jessica would have grabbed his arm if he had opened the door while she was still beside him. He had to wait till it was her turn to get out on the other side. She stood up now and squeezed past all the other legs to go. Silently he opened the left-hand door and dropped lightly to the ground.

The highwayman had chosen a point where bushes had been allowed to grow up close to the verge. They afforded some slight cover as Dan stole forward, past the rear horses, past the leaders, till he had an unbroken view of the highwayman, still as a mounted statue, a brace of pistols levelled in menace.

This had to be the moment. Pray God the Welshman would not shoot the driver. In a commanding voice that would have filled a theatre he shouted, 'Drop your pistols! You're surrounded on all sides!'

He ducked just in time as the first pistol blazed and the bullet went through the branches overhead.

'Aim at his horse!' he yelled. 'We want this man alive!'

There was, of course, no obedient volley from his non-existent companions. But there was no time for Morgan to take in that reassuring fact. The quick-witted coachman had been swift to seize his chance. He had got hold of his blunderbuss and levelled it. There was a deafening explosion as he pulled the trigger.

The next sound was the thunder of hoofs as the highwayman fled for his life.

They reached Bath without further incident. One of the actors, with more experience than Dan of handling a heavy blunderbuss, rode beside the driver for the rest of the journey. It was generally agreed that young Mr Carnaby had done enough – nay, more than enough.

Nine

Dan's father had been right about future delays over their letters. His next reached Mr Widdowson's office by a roundabout route, after a long time in transit.

'*The closure of our port is very awkward,*' he wrote. '*I took care fortunately that none of our vessels was caught in Boston when it happened, so they can ply between other ports anywhere. Most of the other colonies are very sympathetic, but of course they are normally our competitors, so Boston's misfortune could be good luck for New York or Philadelphia. Yet the problem is the same for us all. If we were a single country, not thirteen separate colonies, people would see it more clearly.*'

Dan found that no one in Bath really knew what was happening over there. There might be an occasional paragraph in the press. Items from abroad were listed under the rather odd heading of 'Foreign Intelligence' – which, said Bradley scornfully, would have been more accurately entitled 'Foreign Stupidity'. But Boston was not foreign anyhow. It was British.

Stage folk seldom seemed to read newspapers, unless it was the *Bristol Gazette* or the *Bath Journal* with some reference to the theatre. London newspapers, like the *Morning Post*, could be read in the coffee-houses, but those were places mainly for the local gentry and fashionable visitors who came to take the waters. Dan would have felt like a fish out of water in such company.

Jessica often asked questions about his life in America, but she was completely ignorant about the problems.

'Why should ordinary people like me – in Bath – know anything about it?' she said. 'We've no say in it. It's the King—'

'And Parliament, surely?'

'I suppose so. But not everyone can vote in the elections. I think my father had a vote. I expect my stepfather has: he owns his farm. You need to be a householder, I expect. And if you're a *woman*, like me—' She made a face. 'Who'd want to know a female's opinion?'

Dan could see why so few people had any interest in the London parliament, least of all what orders it sent to the colonies on the other side of the world.

When he did get home (and he was in no hurry to do so), he must explain to people in Boston that they should not be bitter about the British. Their troubles came from King George, himself really no Englishman, for he was mostly German by blood. It was he who appointed their governor. Parliament was run by a clique known as 'the King's Friends' who used it to push through his stiff-necked policies.

Thank goodness his father was not asking him to go home! Quite the opposite, in fact. The ship-owners of Boston were shrewd men of business. They would find ways to outwit this far-off government in London. His father had all the sons he needed to help him. Let Dan proceed with his own venture.

He was getting better parts now. He no longer felt a mere beginner. He could understand how Jessica looked at life – her single-minded deter-mination to fight her way upwards in the world of the theatre. He admired her. But if she could do it, so could he.

He told himself, this Boston business would blow over. It must. Surely it must.

It did not. At last came another letter from home. '*The other colonies are rallying to support us,*' wrote his father. '*They all joined in a gathering at Philadelphia, they called it a continental congress, and every colony but Georgia came. There is to be a*' *general ban on importing British goods. Perhaps that will bring the King to his senses.'*

Dan wondered. But an actor's life left him too little time to think about other things.

They were reviving a blank-verse tragedy, *Venice Preserved*, written over ninety years ago but popular ever since.

'And the author died destitute, straight afterwards, at only thirty-three!' said Bradley cynically. 'But that's the theatre all over!'

Dan had only a small part. He was one of fifteen men in a plot to overthrow the republic of Venice. He doubled this with a footman's role, with no lines at all to speak.

Jessica had been luckier (if you can call it luck, he told himself disgustedly). There were only two women's parts worth having, and she had the second of them – Aquilina, a glamorous Greek woman with a sharp tongue and loose morals. She had an elderly senator in hot pursuit of her. He was too rich for her to run very fast.

Dan hated to see her playing this part: 'Those scenes are *bawdy*,' he complained. 'Not fit for a girl like you! So coarse.'

She tried to soothe him. 'Mr Ruddock speaks most of the worst lines.' The role of the old senator was ideal for the comedian. He was enjoying himself immensely.

'But you have to hear them! Stand on the open stage and listen.'

'I can't help having ears, can I?' she laughed. 'And that's why I can't pretend I didn't know most of the words before I met the play. I grew up in the country, remember.'

Otway had been writing in the reign of Charles II, when plays were more outspoken. Nowadays they were becoming more refined. Some old pieces were being rewritten and cleaned up. *Venice Preserved* was often revived with the cruder scenes cut out.

Dan had to admit that Ruddock was a very good actor, if very immoral as the dirty-minded Antonio. If another girl had been playing Aquilina, he would have roared with laughter like the rest.

It was on one of the nights in Bristol that Dan noticed the mysterious stranger.

There were two reasons why the man aroused his interest. He was doubling his conspirator's part with that of Aquilina's footman, who had little to do but stand still and stare out into the auditorium. He could hardly fail to notice that one box had only a single occupant. Youngish and, so far as the lighting revealed, elegantly dressed. A man-about-town, and the town more likely to be London than Bristol.

That was nothing. More riveting was the way the fellow kept his gaze intent on Jessica – even when she was not speaking or making the slightest move. Even when some other character was delivering a dozen or more lines of blank verse. The stranger's eyes scarcely strayed elsewhere for a moment.

Well, why not? Natural enough, thought Dan. Jessica was worth looking at, wasn't she? If *he'd* been a stranger himself, seeing her for the first time, he'd probably have been just as lost in admiration.

Jessica was his friend. He was pleased for her, proud when he saw the effect she had on strangers. But, as the evening wore on, bringing further chances to observe the man's concentration, he began to resent it a little, perhaps even fear it.

They reached the big scene where the old senator arrived at Aquilina's house shortly before midnight. She, expecting her real lover, was desperate to get rid of him. She told her maid to turn him out: 'I had rather meet a toad in my dish than that old hideous animal in my chamber tonight!'

Jessica was good when the part required her to switch to a mood of pitiless fury. Ruddock was equally effective when he had to play the utter fool: 'Nicky Nacky, I am come, little Nicky, past eleven o'clock, a late hour—'

'I am sick of you – you are an old, silly, impertinent coxcomb, crazy in your head—'

The audience was loving it. They roared with laughter when Ruddock pretended to be a dog and got under the table, shouting 'Bow, wow, wow!' The gallery cheered when Jessica seized a dog-whip and drove him off the stage.

Some comic relief seemed excusable in this dark tragedy. Before the final curtain, the hero would stab his best friend and then commit suicide, the heroine would go mad and die of a broken heart. Even Aquilina, having lost the man she really loved, would take a dagger to her hated old senator. She herself was one of the very few characters to survive. Dan was sentenced to the gallows like the other fourteen conspirators.

This was the last performance of the play they had to give. Tomorrow, in Bath, it would be *The Recruiting Officer*, with Jessica as Silvia in one of her favourite breeches parts. It would be Dan's own first appearance in this comedy, a good chance to shine as the wily Sergeant Kite. He welcomed an opportunity to play an older man. It was more challenging.

Rumbling home that night – the two caterpillars drove close together now, to discourage any further encounter with highwaymen – he asked Jessica if she had been troubled by the mysterious stranger.

'The *what*?' she whispered back.

'That young man, you must have noticed. He sat in a box all by himself. He noticed *you*. Never took his eyes off. I thought – I wondered – you might have been disturbed—'

She smothered a laugh. 'I swear, Dan, I wasn't aware of anything. I happened to be *acting*. I had other things to concentrate on. I couldn't be gawping at individual members of the audience. Perhaps I should be flattered. Should I?'

He wished he had not said anything. The man's expression had hardly been one of sentimental admiration. It had been, well, not critical, but intently observant. They murmured amiable gossip for the rest of the journey.

Dan had not, however, seen the last of the mysterious stranger. They had not left him behind in Bristol. He was at Orchard Street the following evening. Not in a box, but this time in the crowded pit.

Ruddock peeped through the curtains at the gathering audience. 'Ah, he's with us again. Spotted him last night.'

'Do you know him?'

'Everyone in this business knows Henry Bate.'

'Wonder who he's after this time,' said Bradley.

Dan felt confirmed in his suspicions of the previous evening. The stranger was some immoral young man of fashion in London who went after attractive girls – especially young actresses who were thought to be fair game, and often were. Well, he would be disappointed if he imagined Jessica—surely he *would* be disappointed, thought Dan desperately, but he must be strongly attracted if he had pursued her all the way to Bath.

It was under this misapprehension that he carelessly answered Bradley, 'Well, you can be sure he won't be after you. Or Mr Ruddock.'

Luckily they had moved away from their peephole and could talk in ordinary tones.

'And why not?' demanded Bradley, suddenly indignant. 'Don't be too certain. Mr Ruddock's talents are widely recognised. And I, though I say it myself—'

Dan was covered with confusion. 'I misunderstood. I only meant that, as obviously you weren't either of you young *girls*, he wouldn't be after you—'

Apparently Mr Bate was doing only what their own Mr Palmer did, quite respectably, when he toured other towns: looking for fresh talent he could attract to his own playhouse.

'You mean he owns a theatre?'

'No. But he's a personal friend of Mr Garrick – the great Mr Garrick, of Drury Lane. You might say that Mr Bate's *bait* is an offer from Drury Lane!'

Bradley cackled at his own pun. Dan was less amused. The stranger was a more serious threat now that he was explained. It had seemed incredible that Jessica would be taken in by the advances of some unknown seducer. But a genuine offer from Drury Lane, the height of every actress's ambition . . . Could she resist a temptation like that? And why should she?

If she were whisked away to London, he would be left without a friend in Bath.

The call-boy's cry broke in on these tumultuous thoughts.

'*Beginners, please!*' He must take hold of himself, forget everything but his lines, become Sergeant Kite. And, when the play forced him to meet

Jessica face to face, he must see nobody but the magistrate's daughter, Silvia.

He did his best. But when the final curtain fell, Dan knew he had not given the performance he had hoped to give.

He waited for the girl to come out of the ladies' dressing-room. Should he say anything in that brief walk to their lodgings? Had she herself been told anything yet? Was there going to be anything to tell? Or was it a false alarm, prompted by the casual words of Bradley and Ruddock?

It was hard to forget the stranger's behaviour last night. His concentration on Jessica . . .

Until tonight Dan had not realised how important the girl's friendship had become to him. There was no 'understanding' between them. How could there be? She was always emphatic: she would not think of husbands and children till she was securely established in her career. And he himself had come from America, and would go back there as soon as he had mastered his craft. And, in the nature of things, it would be even longer before *he* could think of taking on a wife.

He looked forward eagerly to the few minutes they would have together as they walked to Abbey Green. He had still not decided whether to raise the question himself, when she emerged from the dressing-room and came in his direction. She was following at the heels of the call-boy, who was heading for Mr Palmer's office.

She did not stop, just slackened her steps, smiled up at him, and murmured almost soundlessly, 'Don't wait. Mr Palmer—' A minute later the call-boy returned and said discreetly, 'Mrs Stone sends her apologies, Mr Carnaby. Someone will see her safely home.'

After that he could hardly linger. But when he reached his own door he hesitated to go in. For once, he felt no eagerness for the cold supper Mrs Askew would have set out for him. Healthy boyish appetite had been replaced by – what? Manly something, he told himself with forced humour.

He must be sensible. Mr Palmer had sent for Jessica after the performance. That could mean anything . . . or nothing. It certainly need not be anything to do with this Mr Bate. Anyhow, she had to obey the summons. She had sent him that reassuring message, he was not to wait, someone would see her safely home. And reason told him that someone would. He could rely on Mr Palmer. If he had to escort her himself, Mr Palmer would never leave her to walk through the streets alone at that hour.

But Dan's mind remained in a turmoil. At one moment he vowed, I'm not going in till I see her safely delivered to her door. At another, he told himself not to be a fool. Suppose she did not come; maybe for some perfectly respectable reason? He might be locked out of his own lodgings all night. Any minute now Bradley and Ruddock would come lurching home. He did not want to explain himself to them.

Ah! Footsteps on the flagstone, orderly footsteps, definitely not those of the two comedians. And quiet voices, also *certainly* not theirs.

One tree grew in the middle of the square. Dan moved into its shadows. A man's voice was saying, 'Of course you must have time to think it over, Mrs Stone. As you see, Mr Palmer will leave you free to decide.'

'I am honoured, Mr Bate. Tomorrow we play in Bristol. May I give you my decision the next morning?'

'Of course, dear lady. Take your time. I have friends in Bath. And the Pelican is most comfortable.'

They parted with decorum. The door closed behind her. The stranger, no longer mysterious, strode cheerfully away.

Dan slipped quietly into his own lodgings and

attacked his delayed supper with sudden ferocity.

Tomorrow being a Bristol day, they were all to parade to the caterpillars soon after noon. Their early call at Orchard Street was very brief.

Jessica pounced upon him. 'I'm sorry about last night! Mr Palmer sent for me—'

'The call-boy told me. So I did not worry,' he lied. She must not know how anxiously he had spied on her and eavesdropped on that little farewell scene with Mr Bate.

'It was your mysterious stranger,' she said excitedly. 'Mr Bate. He seemed most respectable. Think! He had come down from London to see my Silvia. He has made me an offer – Drury Lane! London! He is a personal friend of the great Mr Garrick. Can you believe it?'

Only too well, he thought. Keeping his voice steady he said, 'And will you accept it?'

'I've promised to consider it.'

'Consider it? I thought any actress would jump at Drury Lane.'

She laughed. 'Of course! At least *I* shall. I should be crazy not to. But it doesn't always pay to seem too eager. To hesitate might be worth another pound a week.'

'You are a cunning little devil,' he said. 'But it will be dull in Bath without you.'

'Oh, Dan, I shall miss you too.'

It came to him in a flash what he must do. Instantly. 'I must go,' he said. 'We can talk on the way to Bristol.'

'Of course! Keep a seat for me. Isn't it *wonderful*?'

'It certainly is. I *do* congratulate you.' Even Mr Bate could not have sounded more correct.

Ten

Once out of the girl's sight, he lost his calm. He strode off as though he had made a bet on some athletic challenge. He must catch Mr Bate at once, before boarding the caterpillar for Bristol.

Jessica was giving her answer tomorrow morning. She had not told Dan so, but he had overheard her promise Mr Bate last night. Then, very likely the man would be gone, back to London or elsewhere. It would be too late.

Dan must find him within the next two or three hours. And Jessica must never know.

He was breathless, almost speechless, when he reached the Pelican.

'Mr Bate?' echoed the maid he asked. 'Oh no, sir. I'm afraid you're unlucky, sir. You've just missed him.'

Hell, thought Dan. The man has friends in Bath. He would. He'll be spending the day with them. 'Do you know when he will be back?' he inquired with little hope.

Another maid joined in. 'I heard him say he

was just taking a stroll along the river. Probably back quite soon. If you'd care to take a seat in the garden, sir—'

'Thank you. I can perhaps catch up with him—' He was off like a bloodhound on the scent.

Mr Bate had gone upstream, out of town and away from the noise of the workmen on Pulteney Bridge. The towpath soon led to the open country, steep sloping meadows and patches of woodland offering welcome shade. Later in the day it would be a promenade for visitors. As early as this, it was deserted . . . except for the elegant Mr Bate, who had sat down against a tree and was reading a book.

This was luck indeed. Seen for the first time in broad daylight, the man hardly looked a mysterious stranger. He had a cheerful, full-blooded face, and was powerfully built.

Dan slackened speed and braced himself for the effort he must make.

'Pah!' exclaimed Mr Bate suddenly. He slapped his book shut with a contemptuous gesture and thrust it into his pocket. Then, hearing Dan's footsteps, he looked up and smiled. 'A pleasant morning, young man!'

'Yes, indeed, sir. Especially here, with the river—'

'Most welcome, the river, when I've landed myself with a damnably dry book!' Dan laughed politely. 'But the *Morning Post* wants me to write a piece. Peace? There can be no peace between me and the fool who wrote *that*. I shall demolish him.'

Mr Bate's face contorted with comical fury. Was this the suave-spoken shadow he had overheard conversing with Jessica last night? The tone changed again: 'Haven't I seen you before somewhere?'

Dan seized his chance. 'Possibly, sir. In the theatre?'

'I was there last night. And Bristol the night before. A good-looking young footman? In *Venice Preserved*.'

It was not very flattering to be remembered for his non-speaking part. He must not let resentment creep into his voice. 'And I was Sergeant Kite in *The Recruiting Officer*,' he said.

'Were you now? Odd casting, that. I remember now – feeling it should have been played by an older man. Still,' Mr Bate conceded, 'you did your best. And with time, no doubt . . .'

Things were not going well. Dan changed his tack. 'Excuse me, sir. I was told that the famous

Mr Bate was in the house last night – forgive the familiarity, but is it possible that you—' He opened his eyes wider to signify amazement.

'I am certainly Mr Bate. Famous . . . or infamous? Opinions vary.'

Dan plunged. 'I was wondering, sir—' Desperately he poured out his ambitions to get to London. Could Mr Bate advise him? Could Mr Bate *help* him?

'It's a praiseworthy ambition,' his companion admitted. 'But are you not rather young? Should you not wait a little, gain more experience?' There was, he added, keen competition to get work with the Drury Lane company or with its rival, Covent Garden. Bath was an excellent theatre. Did he realise how fortunate he was? What's the hurry, Mr Bate demanded, with a sign of growing impatience.

Dan knew that he was at a disadvantage, because he was not telling the exact truth. At all costs he must get to Drury Lane. He could not face the future in Bath without Jessica. It was the one reason he could not possibly give. He explained that he had come over from Boston with this dream of learning an actor's trade in the country best known for it; how vital it obviously was to see the great playhouses of

London. All true enough, up to a point. But somehow unconvincing at this moment when his mind was full of other considerations.

Mr Bate was sympathetic but he could run short of patience with persistent young men who would not take no for an answer. Dan sensed his reaction, knew that he was getting nowhere. Sick at heart, he saw that if he went on any longer Mr Bate would lose his patience. He stood up, thanked him for his advice, and started on his way back. He must get a bite to eat and then it would be time to think of Bristol.

He was so deep in gloom that he did not notice the two approaching figures until they were almost upon him. He stepped aside hastily. They were both burly, unkempt characters. One, answering some remark from his companion, twisted his features contemptuously to pronounce the one word, '*Naouw!*' After what followed Dan could guess the question he was answering. They were not men one would wish to meet on a dark night.

That thought prompted another. He looked back. The men were approaching Mr Bate, who had returned to the study of his dull book. He waited to make sure that the men passed on their way. They did not. He saw Mr Bate jump to his feet. The three figures suddenly blurred together, struggling to and fro on the towpath. Something black – Mr Bate's hat probably – went flying.

Dan rushed back. Angry voices rang through the air. There seemed little chance that any one else would hear. The landscape was empty. No one else was likely to intervene. He must do what he could.

One of the men saw him. He bellowed a coarse instruction which was seldom heard in polite Boston circles. Dan ignored it, and hurtled on, fists clenched. A massive hairy chest loomed; two powerful arms gripped him in a bearlike embrace. He could see nothing but ragged jacket and human flesh. His feet had been swept off the ground.

'Let the lad go!' cried Mr Bate.

The grip loosened. Dan felt the path firm again under his feet. He staggered and straightened up, recovering his balance. He was in time to see Mr Bate's fist connect with the man's jaw. The fellow yelped and went sailing backwards through the air, to land in the river behind him with an almighty splash.

His companion was picking himself up from the ground and returning to the struggle. Mr Bate swung round.

'You want to take the waters, too? You could do with it!'

Out streaked the clenched fist. How odd it looked, thrust from the cuff of delicate lace, but how decisive when it made contact and a second spread-eagled scoundrel met the water. His bedraggled companion was already floundering towards the bank. Neither made any sign of returning to the fray. They were lost quickly in the landscape.

Mr Bate picked up his hat, brushed some dust off it, and said, 'I hope you are not hurt? It was good of you to return to the rescue.'

'It was *you* rescued *me*, sir,' Dan insisted.

'We will not argue. You will join me in a drink at the Pelican?'

Dan could not refuse, although conscious that his performance had not been very effective. Time was slipping by. He must on no account miss the Bristol call aboard the caterpillar. They had their drink together at the inn without any further mention of his playhouse dreams.

A day or two later, after he had recounted the incident to his fellow-lodgers, Bradley roared with appreciative laughter.

'That's just like the Fighting Parson!'

'The what?'

'The Fighting Parson.'

'You don't mean that Mr Bate is—'

With the help of their landlady the two comedians explained how different some English ministers of religion were from their brethren in the American colonies. English parsons were not dependent for their livelihood on the congregations they ministered to. Their churches probably had endowments of money left whole centuries ago.

'We talk of "livings",' said Mrs Askew. 'The parson can be appointed to it – by the bishop, or whoever owns it. Mr Bate's father owned his own living at Worcester, and when he died he left it to Mr Bate. Their real surname is Dudley, though.'

Dan stared, and stared even more as she went on.

Mr Bate did not want to be a parson but he wanted the money. As he had been to Oxford or Cambridge it was only a formality to 'take Holy Orders' and become 'the Reverend'. He need not take services or perform any other duties; he need only hire a substitute, a curate, for a tiny salary, and go off to London himself to lead the very different kind of life he fancied.

'So he *is* a parson,' said Bradley. 'And he's a fighting parson because he loves a rough-and-tumble – he's a match for most of the professional prizefighters. But he's always game for a proper duel if he gets the chance.'

'And *I* went to rescue *him*!' Dan exclaimed, shame-faced, but laughing at the same time.

By then he had recovered the power to laugh over the whole episode. Mr Bate had departed to London in triumph, having secured Jessica's acceptance of the Drury Lane contract. But before leaving he had sought out Dan for a private word.

'Ah, Mr Carnaby! I have been thinking. Are you still set on your idea of Drury Lane?'

'Yes, sir! And I swear I'll get there. Sooner or later.'

Mr Bate smiled. 'It could be sooner.'

Dan stared, incredulous.

'I said I knew of no vacancies. But Mr Garrick is always glad to know of a lad of promise. I think if I recommended you, room *could* be found. On a modest rate of pay at first. What do you say?'

'Oh, yes, sir! *Yes!*'

Within the hour he was confiding the news to Jessica. 'I can hardly believe it! He was so positive. No vacancies, so much competition. He hadn't been at all impressed by anything I told him. And, as for that little affair with those men by the river, I didn't do *anything*. It was he who stopped *them* from chucking *me* into the water.'

'I expect it *was* that.' She seemed to be trying hard to convince him. But, as he was learning, she might be a first-class actress but she was a very poor liar. It was a long time afterwards that he discovered what a decisive part she had played in Mr Bate's surprising change of mind.

Eleven

For a day or two Jessica's offer from Drury Lane was the talk of the company. There was a little jealousy, of course. Wild hopes had stirred in many a mind once the word got round that the famous Mr Bate had been in the house two nights running. But Jessica was popular, and once people realised that the good luck was not to be theirs, their congratulations were genuine. She had talent, news of it had penetrated to London, and Mr Bate had come down specially to see her . . . She would go far. She deserved to.

As to the offer made to the young man from America, nobody could make sense of that. Mr Carnaby was good-looking, yes, he had some talent, he was pleasant, with more gentlemanly polish than they would have expected in a colonial. 'I've often said he'd go far,' said one lady, 'but I only meant back to America!'

Most people concluded that he owed the offer to that little episode with the footpads who had attacked Mr Bate by the river. Mr Carnaby was too modest. They remembered the incident of the highwayman. Yes, the young man must have done something brave . . . though he denied it almost with embarrassment. They could imagine no other explanation.

Mr Palmer was very pleasant about it all. He was sad to be losing Jessica; philosophic about Dan. He would, of course, release both of them. Mr Garrick wrote to agree the date when Mrs Stone was to join his company and Mr Carnaby could follow when convenient. Mr Palmer saw no difficulty in releasing Dan on the same date. He would be an escort for Mrs Stone.

'Even the faster coaches still take two days,' he told Dan, 'so you will spend the night at an inn. It is only a hundred miles,' he added scornfully. 'If I had the organising of it all, such a journey could be managed in a day – a long day perhaps, or partly by night. People would be spared the expense of a stop halfway.'

Ten years later, when Dan had to make that journey in the opposite direction, he remembered Palmer's words and the faraway look in his eyes. Much as Palmer loved his playhouse, he was never just a man of the theatre like Shandy Henderson, who worked himself to an early death there. Palmer had other dreams. In the years ahead he was to work out a scheme for speeding up the

Royal Mail by taking it out of the hands of the post boys and passing it over to a national network of mail-coaches which would carry both letters and passengers at speeds unknown before. The government put him in charge of it – and it worked.

All that still lay in the future, a mere gleam in Palmer's eye. When Dan and Jessica set out on their journey together they stopped at Newbury overnight, supping with their fellow-passengers and sleeping in different wings of a rambling old inn.

Jessica paused at the top of the stairs and turned. 'We part here, then,' she said cheerfully. 'A long day! But how good to spend it together. And now at least to be under the same roof—'

The phrase struck an echo in Dan's mind. An answer sprang to his lips, but it occurred to him that it might seem to her slightly improper, so he choked it back in a burst of confused laughter.

'What?' she demanded.

'N–nothing! Really. I – I just remembered—'

'Out with it!'

'A saying of Mrs Askew. Why she would never take young lady lodgers as well as young gentle-men.' He imitated her prim accents: 'They start by pleading that they just want to share the same roof, but in no time you find they meant ceiling.'

He was relieved by her frank laughter. But her answer caught Mrs Askew's prim tone exactly: 'I think it is high time we said goodnight, Mr Carnaby.' She tilted her face. Her eyes danced in the candlelight. 'No,' she said a moment later, 'that will do well enough on the *stage*—'

They must have kissed so often in plays, they were naturally cast so frequently in parts which called for it. Such kisses were unreal, with no feeling. Tonight she clearly wanted something different. He responded with a thrill of delight, till she broke away decisively and picked up her candle again from the table at the head of the stairs. 'We must not set ourselves on fire,' she said lightly. But she was almost dancing as she vanished down the corridor.

He had looked forward to this two-day journey. He would be discovering England, he told himself. So far, he had seen nothing but Bristol and Bath. The road to London took them right across the country, with even a distant glimpse of the great Windsor Castle on its hill, from which the tiresome King George issued the orders that so vexed Dan's father and the other people back home. But, by the end of the second day, he realised that he had learnt not only a great deal about England but something fresh about himself. And this girl, Jessica.

You *are* stupid, Daniel Carnaby, he told himself critically. Anyone in their senses would have *realised* . . .

From that first rehearsal they had been drawn together in an easy natural friendship. They shared a sense of humour, she had taught him elementary things about the theatre and English ways in general, she seemed interested (which was flattering) when he answered her questions about America.

And surely, all those *plays*! Tragic or comic, they were nearly all concerned with love. The characters often thought of little else. Why should he imagine that he was any different – that sooner or later he too would not be caught up in such emotions? Yet he had only begun to realise it when Mr Bate came on the scene, and the thought of Jessica vanishing to London had become unbearable. And now Jessica's goodnight at the inn. Was he imagining too much, or was she beginning to feel the same?

They reached London in the early evening of that second day. They were to report to Mr Garrick the next morning. Lodgings had been arranged for them on arrival, which they would be free, of course, to alter later. For the moment, though, Mr Garrick had booked their rooms to save them trouble, arriving as unknown strangers in an overcrowded city.

They felt thankful for this as the coach covered its final mile along the busy streets and swung into the cobbled yard of the inn which served as terminus. An eager porter pounced on their assorted baggage and led the way.

It was not far to Drury Lane. Drury Court, where Jessica was to stay, proved to be a little side-turning close to the great theatre itself, where the evening performance sounded as if it were in progress. 'It will be very handy for you,' said Dan enviously. 'I think my Mrs Askew must have selected our lodgings!'

'Mrs Askew?' She looked puzzled. 'Oh, I remember – your rather proper landlady on Abbey Green! Where did you say your room was?'

'Bolt Court. It's off Fleet Street. Some way from here – in the other direction!'

'Never mind!' She smiled. 'I expect we shall meet.'

'We'd better. Tomorrow. Nine o'clock sharp.'

They knocked on the door. He handed in her bags. They exchanged secret smiles but not kisses. The servant was not to get any wrong ideas.

A hundred years ago, it was said, Nell Gwyn had lodged there, and carried on her love affair with King Charles II. It was now a most respectable establishment. 'Anyhow,' Jessica had assured Dan, 'I have no wicked ambition to carry on that tradition with our present sovereign.' And they both laughed at the thought of her – or anyone else – misbehaving with the highly respectable George III.

It was in fact no more than half a mile to Dan's lodgings. Now that they were alone, and Dan walked beside him, the porter became talkative. It was a good house he was going to, well-kept and decent. Tim Blagg had been a scene-shifter till his injury. Mr Garrick did not forget people who had worked well for him. The young gentleman would be comfortable.

They followed the Lane till it ended in the Strand, then swung left, past a massive gatehouse, Temple Bar, and into Fleet Street. 'We're in the old city now, sir. All this part was burnt down in the Great Fire, more than a hundred years ago.' It seemed to have been built up again higgledy-piggledy, not at all like Bath. And the narrow side-turnings led to an even worse confusion. At last they reached a small square, Gough Square, and Bolt Court was one of its tiny alleys. 'Very central, sir,' said the porter.

Tim Blagg was a tall man with a decided limp but a ready smile. He led the way upstairs to an attic with two beds. 'Hope you don't mind, sir. Had to put you in with young Mr Digby for the time being. You don't know him? Oh, you soon will: young actor at the Lane, sir, same as yourself. I'm afraid it's "House Full" here, same as it is there!'

Dan did not mind sharing, at least for a time. It would be useful, possibly pleasant, to have some young male company. It would be an economy, too. Though Jessica had been offered a useful increase in salary, he himself had not. He was a little worried about the cost of living in London.

It was a matter of pride not to fall back on the help his father had offered. He was determined to set his teeth and exist on this venture on what he could earn: it was not going to end in humiliating failure. Anyhow, things seemed to be getting more and more difficult in this drawn-out dispute between the people at home and the London government. It might become impossible to transmit money from Boston to England.

'Mrs Blagg wondered, sir – you will have had a long day on the road – she could quickly provide a simple meal—'

Dan accepted gratefully. Pausing only to wash his hands and face, unpack his nightshirt and toss it on to the bed indicated, he hurried downstairs.

The sun was setting when he rose from the table. He thought of Jessica. What would she be doing? Gossiping with congenial ladies? Making little feminine preparations for her interview with the mighty Mr Garrick tomorrow? Or – just possibly – missing him?

He could hardly go to bed yet. He would stretch his legs while the light lasted. He must see a little of London, the city he had dreamed of.

He made his way back to Fleet Street and continued eastwards along the stretch he had not yet seen. The street curved down slightly to an evil-smelling stream, then rose again steeply, filling the eastern sky with a huge domed building which must be the famous cathedral of St Paul. He quickened his pace up the hill. Now he was seeing the London he had heard of.

He walked round the outside. It was getting dark. He must come back in daylight when he could go inside. Christopher Wren's masterpiece, after that fire. His mother would want a full description.

He turned down a sidestreet that brought him

to the riverbank. The Thames was crowded with boats and barges passing to and fro, with many smaller craft steering a skilful course across the main traffic merely to the opposite bank. That southern side looked densely built-up. To get across by bridge meant a long detour, so people must use ferries or hire watermen.

He had better turn back. London at night, he had been warned, was no place for a lone stranger to get lost. But he had got here. He would sleep tonight in legendary London. And from tomorrow he would belong to the renowned company of Drury Lane.

There was a golden line of candlelight under his bedroom door. Gilbert Digby turned to greet him with outstretched hand. He was only a year or two older than Dan, tallish, dark and good-looking, with an assured voice and manner – a London polish, thought Dan enviously.

They chatted pleasantly as they undressed. Dan apologised for his intrusion on Digby's privacy.

'No intrusion, my dear fellow! Someone to talk to! I shall show you the ropes. The sights of London Town.'

Dan thanked him. 'I've seen St Paul's cathedral already,' he said, to show that he was not one to waste time.

He could not understand why the young actor laughed so loudly. 'I had in mind a rather different kind of sight,' he said. But he did not explain.

Twelve

It was good to meet Jessica at the theatre next morning, and to compare notes in undertones while they waited to see Mr Garrick.

She seemed happy in her new quarters and with the actresses she had met. Jessica had a room to herself, but thought Dan lucky to be sharing with someone like Digby. 'You need a friend,' she said. 'I mean a man friend. And someone young like yourself; not like those old comics in Bath!'

They stared round, as they waited. Inside, the theatre was impressive. It had just been completely remodelled and redecorated.

'By Robert Adam himself,' she said.

'Who's he?'

'Of course, you wouldn't know. He's the most famous architect in London. He's designed so many of the finest buildings – architect to the King—'

Dan looked round the auditorium with due respect. It was pale green, pink and bronze. It must have held about two thousand. The apron-stage, stretching forward from the curtain, was vast in itself.

A voice broke in on their whisperings. 'Mrs Stone? Mr Garrick will see you now.'

'Good luck.' He could not imagine that she would need it. He was the one who did. Jessica had a growing reputation which had brought Bate all the way to Bath and earned her this contract. She would justify it and go on now from strength to strength. His own presence here, however, was still rather a mystery. Some whim of Bate's perhaps? An impulsive change of mind, going against the reasoned verdict he had first given? Well, it was up to Dan now to prove himself.

He had learnt a lot at Bath; he was no longer a beginner. Henderson had been an inspiring example. Even the 'old comics' had taught him professional tricks that helped one to survive on the punishing treadmill of ever-changing parts. But this sudden move to London had lifted him out of his class a little too soon.

At last Jessica was at his elbow again. She looked as though her interview had gone well. 'Mr Garrick said to send you in,' she murmured. Her lips framed, rather than spoke, the awed words she added: 'He is *wonderful*!'

Dan walked down the passage, tapped on the

door, and went in, bowing to the man who rose to greet him.

'Mr Carnaby?'

'At your service, sir.'

At first sight David Garrick was almost a disappointment. Dan had heard so much about him. The man's reputation had prepared him for a more impressive – even overpowering – figure. In appearance he was quite small, under average height, sixty-ish and beginning to put on weight. Was this the giant of the English theatre people spoke of?

Dan's disappointment quickly vanished. The man was so intensely alive. He had a piercing eye and mobile features. Dan remembered he was of French origin, descendant of those Huguenots who had sought refuge from religious persecution at home. Mr Garrick had grown up in the English Midlands and come to London as a youth to seek his fortune – legend said with no more than a penny ha'penny in his pocket. His first performance, as Richard III, had made him famous overnight. That was many years ago, and he had never looked back.

'Mr Bate tells me you come from America?'

'Yes, sir. From Boston.'

'Is there a playhouse there?'

'No, sir – not yet.' Dan spoke the last two words with determination. There would be, if he had to found it *himself*. He would work on his father to put up the money.

'Then how did you come to—' Garrick paused, eyeing him with curiosity.

Dan told him of his visit to New York. How it had revealed to him what could be done by bringing Shakespeare's plays to life on a stage.

Garrick responded with enthusiastic agreement. I *did* pick on the right line to take with him, Dan told himself with triumph. The man's passion for Shakespeare was famous. In his thirty-odd years of managing Drury Lane, he had put on most of the plays. He had rescued them from the dreadfully distorted versions that the public had been given for generations. He was so devoted to the memory of the playwright that he had organised a great festival, only a few years ago, to honour him at his birthplace, a little town called Stratford.

'You can speak his blank verse?' demanded Garrick anxiously.

'I do my best, sir.' The older actors at Bath had told Dan how Garrick had transformed the delivery of Shakespeare's lines, as indeed he had revolutionised so much else. The tradition of

121

declaiming them pompously had been abandoned. You spoke them in natural tones, varying your pace as if you were voicing your own thoughts and emotions, not merely reciting a set piece you had learnt by heart.

'We are about to revive *The Merchant*,' said Garrick. Dan's heart leapt with a wild hope. 'Let me see what you can do.' The manager picked up a book, opened it, and held it out. 'Be so good, Mr Carnaby.'

Dan saw with disappointment that it was open at the scene where the Prince of Aragon comes as suitor for the hand of Portia and fails the casket test by pointing to the silver one. It was not a long scene, but the Prince's lines took up most of it. They would challenge any actor's skill to hold the unbroken attention of his audience. He must not recite, he must be thinking the words as they came to his lips . . .

Garrick stopped him before the end. 'That will do, excellently. You have the right idea.' He took back the book. 'Come this afternoon and ask to see the wardrobe master. He must find something worthy of a prince. Or have it made. I hope you will be very happy with us, young man.'

Dan found himself out in the passage. Jessica was waiting for him. Eager. Perhaps a little anxious.

'How did it go?'

'Well enough . . . I think. I have a part, anyhow.'

'In *The Merchant*?'

Yes. The Prince of Aragon.'

'Not—?' Her face fell. 'I'd hoped—'

'So did I, for one wild moment,' he admitted. He must not show his disappointment. 'That's too much to expect, though. So you *are* to be Jessica?'

'I – I'm afraid so.' Apology and triumph struggled together in her voice.

He wanted to put a reassuring arm round her waist but he had learnt to control such instincts. 'How wonderful! I'm so glad for you.'

'It is wonderful. But I do wish—'

He laughed. 'We must be reasonable—'

'I'm not *good* at being reasonable.' That was not true, in the ordinary way, he thought.

'We can't expect them to cast the play to suit us. We've not been engaged as a double act! A new part will be good experience for me. A new Lorenzo will be interesting for you.'

Her normal spirits returned. Garrick had cast his spell upon her. The next excitement was the choice of costumes.

Garrick had long ago given up the practice of dressing his casts in the styles of their own day.

They must be costumed appropriately for the country and century concerned, Venice or Vienna, Cleopatra's Egypt or Caesar's Rome. When Jessica dropped from her balcony she would wear doublet and hose.

Hundreds of costumes hung ready for choice. Skilful tailors and seamstresses would adjust the fitting if necessary or a completely fresh garment would be made. Old or new, each carried a label declaring that it was the 'Property of the Management'. The word had become almost a joke: whatever object was needed onstage, cushion or cup or crown, was referred to as a 'property'.

Dan, as a Spanish prince, was thought worthy of the most impressive costume he had ever worn. 'You look *wonderful*,' Jessica assured him. 'Scarlet and silver! And that cloak! If it were real life, Portia would be wild when you chose the wrong casket. If she'd been quick-witted enough she'd have given you a secret signal so you'd pick the right one.'

'Would *you*?'

'Well, what do *you* think?'

She as Jessica, Shylock's daughter, must not wear anything so showy. Only for that last glorious scene in the moonlit garden would she change into a superbly sweeping blue gown that set off her face and figure.

But she would share that scene with someone else. That evening he discovered it would be with Digby. Fortunately she took to him, and he to her.

'He's a good sort,' Dan assured her as warmly as he could.

'I'm sure he is! Of course I wish it could have been you. But as you said then, we must be reasonable.'

Digby was equally approving. As he and Dan undressed in their attic that night, he said, 'A nice little filly!'

'You think so?' Dan did not much like the familiar way Digby referred to her. 'Filly' was meant favourably but it grated. Jessica was not a horse, even of the most attractive kind. She was not a four-legged creature. Two legs, of *her* sort, were enough.

'Of course you were at Bath together, weren't you?' Digby's tone was casual but Dan guessed he was fishing for information. 'Did you . . . get on well?'

'We are very good friends,' he told Digby. He climbed into bed. 'Goodnight,' he said pleasantly, but in a tone that firmly closed the conversation.

Over the next few days Dan enlarged his acquaintance with the Drury Lane company until he felt he knew almost everybody, from its mighty manager down to the theatre staff like Johnston the boxkeeper, and his immense dog (Garrick called it 'Bear') with which he guarded the premises.

Garrick himself was not in the cast. He acted only occasionally nowadays. There were alarming rumours that he might soon retire. He had made a fortune, he had moved into a house beside the Thames at Hampton, he was happily married to a former dancer from Vienna (Violette, said to be best of women and wives), though they had not been blessed with children. He was a good age now, but there seemed to be no failing in his health and vitality.

'I think his eye is everywhere,' said Jessica. 'He does not miss things, so look out.'

He was certainly still open to new ideas. In recent years he had introduced many striking improvements in stage lighting, inspired by trips to Paris with his wife. Dan was constantly jotting down such things in a notebook. The dream of one day starting his own theatre in America was growing in his mind. He was determined to learn everything he could.

Though he had only a single scene in this production, it was at least a vital one to the plot. It was a scene with the heroine Portia, he had most of the lines, and while it lasted it was he who really held the stage. It gave him a sensation he had not known before.

The actress playing Portia was little older than Jessica and himself, and had only just come to Drury Lane – another of Mr Bate's recommendations. She seemed vastly older and more experienced, because she had been born into a famous theatrical family, the Kembles, and had toured with her parents from babyhood. At eighteen, she had married – much against their wishes – a second-rate actor, William Siddons, and now had two children. Dan found her a striking figure with her dark eyes and black hair, but Jessica was critical. 'Sarah', she said, 'has done all the wrong things.'

She felt no jealousy. She and Mrs Siddons were not likely to be rivals. Jessica favoured comedy. The older girl leant towards tragedy; she positively disliked the breeches parts in which Jessica excelled. As she confessed privately, she did not care to display her figure. 'And if she goes on having babies,' said Jessica frankly, 'she won't be able to.'

Jessica was more afraid of the competition of Mary Robinson, another recent recruit, whom Garrick himself had been coaching and trying out in light girlish parts. Mary was nineteen and very beautiful. But wild. She had been married at sixteen to an equally wild young man. Very soon afterwards he had landed them both in prison for debt. The unhappy marriage had not lasted, but luckily there had been no babies.

'Mr Garrick thinks she shows promise,' said Jessica. 'I'm sure she does! But promise of what?' Some of the older ladies in the company thought Mary would happily quit the stage if she could catch the roving eye of a rich man, preferably a lord. She would not expect him to marry her.

'Oh, surely—' Dan protested. He could still be shocked by the behaviour of some actresses.

But the cynical judgement of the other ladies was justified in the end. A few years later Mary left the stage for a spell as mistress to a very high-ranking gentleman indeed, the King's eldest son, later to be the Prince Regent, and eventually King himself, as George IV.

It was quite an education, working at Drury Lane.

Mrs Frances Abington regarded herself as the leading lady, though she was taking no part in

The Merchant. She had started life as a flower-seller and street-singer, and had refined her speech and manners by working for a milliner. Garrick disliked her, but admitted that she had developed into a first-class actress. And there was Jane Pope, who would once have been Jessica's most formidable rival in the pert young lady parts but was now too old and plump for them. She had sensibly carved herself a second career in elderly roles, and, had they but known, would still be acting thirty years later.

The men in the company were just as interesting in their various ways. There was Mr Dodd, who excelled in character parts like foolish dandies, but offstage was studious and middle-aged with a great love of books. There was a John Palmer, no connection with the one at Bath, but son of the pit door-keeper at Drury Lane. Garrick had seen his talent and he had justified the opportunity given him.

In contrast there was William Smith, rather grand and more often referred to as 'Gentleman' Smith. He was handsome and elegant, had been to Eton and Cambridge, and was very conscious of his own dignity. He would never act in a farce, or black his face, or come onstage through a trapdoor for comic effect.

He was such a fine actor, though, that Garrick accepted these conditions. Indeed, he shared with him some of his own famous parts, like Hamlet and Richard III. Another of Gentleman Smith's terms was that he would never perform on a Monday in the hunting season. He was a keen rider to hounds, pursuing stags or foxes with equal determination.

There was something individual about everyone at the Lane, though poor Sarah Siddons' husband was hardly outstanding. Gilbert Digby, naturally, was the young man of whom Dan saw most.

The first night of *The Merchant* seemed to go well, though Sarah's Portia won little praise from the critics. Only the *Morning Post* was enthusiastic – not surprisingly, for the review was by Mr Bate who had brought her to Drury Lane! Dan felt, quite justifiably, that he had dominated his one scene with her. She was miscast, really. She had not the sly cool humour for Portia. She was too serious. How much better Jessica would have been! But she was needed *as* Jessica, he thought, as he watched the rest of the play from the wings when his own part was finished.

He felt a pang of envy during that exquisite last scene at Belmont. The moonlight effects had been created by the transparency method Garrick had learnt in France. She had never looked lovelier than in that long blue dress. If only he, instead of Digby . . .

As they walked to her lodgings afterwards she must have guessed his thoughts. She murmured, 'I was wishing it was you.'

'Were you?' He restrained his delight and forced himself to say, 'I thought he was very good.'

Though she had been charmed with Digby when they first met, she seemed nowadays less enthusiastic. 'I used to think—' she said – she too was clearly making an effort. 'But no, I won't say a word against Digby. You are his friend, after all.'

They had reached her door. He did not want to talk about Digby. His mind was on prolonging their goodnight.

They played *The Merchant* for several nights. Then it was briefly replaced by a Farquhar comedy. That was the good thing about Drury Lane. A play might be a really outstanding success, might fill the house twenty times, but it was kept in repertory and interchanged with others. Garrick had a big enough company to cast them all. It was much less strain than it had been at Bath: at

Drury Lane, one frequently had a night off.

On one such evening Digby recalled his promise to show Dan the sights of London. 'Vauxhall!' he said. 'We'll have a night at the pleasure gardens. Just what I need. And it's high time *you* saw Vauxhall.'

The Spring Gardens lay south of the river, well upstream. For over a hundred years they had been a favourite place of entertainment for Londoners. 'They've got everything a man could wish for,' Digby promised. The best way to get there was to hire a waterman and cross over in his boat.

It cost a shilling each to go into the pleasure gardens, but from the first moment Dan realised what good value it was. The place was vast. It resounded with the laughter and lively chatter of thousands. Music throbbed in the background. The dusk was gathering but the trees glittered with innumerable coloured lights. It was for all classes, but the quality paraded especially up and down the central avenue of magnificent elms.

'The Prince of Wales comes here,' said Digby. 'He gives supper parties in that pavilion over there.'

They saw Mr Bate, red-faced and rather drunk, laughing and quarrelling with a group of friends. Before the evening was over, Dan felt, he would be the Fighting Parson again. So far, people's behaviour seemed orderly enough. There were some noisy young apprentices but the majority looked decent London folk.

There were sideshows and eating-houses and drinking-places to suit every taste and purse. There were dancers and musicians. There were quieter corners where one could sit down in an arbour. There was a lake and fountains, there were caves and grottoes . . .

Jessica would love this, Dan knew. He unwisely spoke that thought aloud, and Digby took it up with unexpected feeling.

'Mrs Stone is well-named,' he said bitterly. 'Cold – and hard! It's extraordinary: onstage she can be so passionate. But in real life!' He positively snorted. 'I'm not surprised you had no luck with her in Bath!'

Dan listened to him with amazement. He did not contradict him. Anyhow, it depended on what you meant by 'luck'. He could well imagine that Digby had expected much more and had resented Jessica's lack of response. Dan had been careful from the start not to let him know how close his own friendship with her was becoming.

To change the subject he suggested a drink, and perhaps one of those delicious chicken-andham pies for which Vauxhall was famous. Digby agreed readily to the drink. 'A pie later, maybe.' He spoke thickly. 'Before that, though, I want a girl.' He made it sound as though a girl, too, was something to eat.

There were a surprising number of girls, walking slowly up and down in ones and twos. Dan realised suddenly why they were there. He was inexperienced in such matters, but not ignorant. He was surprised at Digby, and then after a few moments' thought not so surprised. Some late nights, boasting as he undressed for bed, Digby liked to hint that he was a sophisticated man-about-town, a lively young dog, ripe for all sorts of wickedness.

They sat down and had their beer. Digby talked on, not facing Dan across the table, but intently studying the young women as they passed by. Dan noticed that they did not avoid his stare as a decent lady would have done, dropping her eyes or turning her head. They smiled. They all seemed to smile.

For the first time Digby looked across at him. 'What about you? Do you feel . . . ?' He paused. 'I could easy fix you up.' He was positively leering.

Afterwards Dan felt ashamed that he had hesitated even for a moment. How could he ever have faced Jessica again if he had yielded to the temptation? But he had been growing up fast lately. He disliked being thought of as a 'mere boy': from time to time his manhood stirred within him – his curiosity and his eagerness to satisfy it.

The thought of Jessica saved him. 'Not tonight.' He put on a knowing voice. 'I don't feel like it.'

'Feel like it?' Digby was not taken in. His tone was mocking. 'I don't think you "feel" anything. You've nothing to feel with.' He nodded to one of the young women. She paused, then came up to their table. Digby rose. She was pretty, she had a ready smile. 'Wait here,' he instructed Dan.

'No. I'll find my own way home.'

'Suit yourself.'

Digby and the woman disappeared down a shadowy path winding away from the lights and music. Dan, awhirl with mixed emotions, started for home.

Thirteen

The somewhat unsavoury memory of that first visit to Vauxhall was soon wiped out by happier developments.

One of Mr Blagg's other lodgers left, and Dan was quick to secure the vacant room. Digby was rather unpleasant about it. Dan offered a reasonable excuse – Mr Garrick was giving him bigger parts so he needed a room to himself. Unfortunately, as he soon realised, they were often parts which might otherwise have gone to Digby.

For that same reason Jessica was delighted. Such parts were frequently involved with her own. In any contact, social or physical, she preferred Dan. 'I'm so glad you're no longer sharing with him! I can speak my mind now. He seemed charming at first, but I soon found he was a dirty devil.'

'You don't surprise me,' said Dan.

Better parts had also brought better pay. London had another advantage over Bath. In Bath, though they had been free to walk about together, the town was so small that everyone knew who they were and could gossip about them. They could not set foot in each other's lodging. Eyebrows would have gone up if they had been seen together in a tavern.

London, however, was vast. There were plenty of respectable establishments where such a pair could take a meal, sometimes with a room to themselves. And there was Vauxhall . . .

At the first opportunity Dan took her to the pleasure gardens. How different that second visit was! She adored the life and gaiety, the lights and the music, as he had known she would. After supper in a little Chinese-style kiosk, they explored the shadowy byways. They were by no means alone, but that did not worry them. They ignored the whispers and laughter in the darkness round them, the pretended protests and the rustlings. They were rustling a little themselves, but in a more or less respectable way.

At last she murmured regretfully, 'I think we'd better stop at that, Dan.' He knew that she was right. 'Let's find that lake again. It's time we had a sensible talk,' she added.

In later days they laughed to think that he had never formally proposed to her, as a gentleman should, though they had often *acted* such scenes, sometimes in eloquent verse. Since their arrival in London they had been gradually drawing even closer. They could not imagine a future apart.

On a seat by the man-made lake, in man-made moonlight worthy of Garrick's Belmont, they got down to the details.

They must not think of getting married for some time. People – Dan's parents certainly – would say he was too young. It was different for a girl. They were almost exactly the same age, Jessica actually two months the elder, but girls often married young, especially if they looked anything like her. The obstacle on her side was her absolute determination to establish herself in the theatre. Dan could be thankful for that. There was less risk of her yielding to some suitor older than himself.

'I'm following the example of Gentleman Smith,' she said with a laugh.

It seemed an odd remark. 'Surely,' he said, '*he* doesn't have to worry for fear he'll start having a baby?'

'Oh, I didn't mean *that*! No. But he's so well-established now that he can choose his parts, and Garrick accepts the fact. Even his refusal to play on Mondays. If I could make myself as in-dispensable as he is, with a big public, Garrick would study my convenience. I could marry and tell him if I was expecting a baby – I'd ask him not to plan any breeches parts for me till I got back my normal figure. The thing is to establish your reputation; so they know that if they don't behave reasonably you can simply leave and go to Covent Garden.'

Two years should be enough, she said confidently. For both of them. He too was going ahead now. 'Yes,' she admitted, 'I *may* have a bias! But everyone else says so as well.'

There was only one cloud on the horizon: the worrying news in letters from home. And not only in those letters. Although the problem was seldom mentioned in their own circle, it was cropping up more in London generally. It was argued about in Parliament and the press and by the merchants who were losing money from the restrictions on trade.

Dan wondered how his family were faring. '*We are managing,*' wrote his father cautiously, lest the letter fell into unfriendly hands. '*The King's Navy cannot be everywhere.*'

He prayed to God, he said, that matters could be sorted out without any violence. More and more English troops were being sent over. A General Gage had set up his headquarters in Boston, his redcoats were like a foreign army occupying a captured city.

Jessica was sympathetic when Dan shared his worries. She loved to hear about his family. She longed to meet them all and was confident that one day she would. 'But will they approve of me?'

'They'll adore you.'

Perhaps, they agreed, when eventually the time to marry came, the ceremony should take place in Boston, a mainly Carnaby affair. Her contact with her mother had weakened sadly these past few years. She had really no other family.

With all this terrible trouble going on and on in the colonies, it was impossible to see the future. Normally they might have found places in a touring company crossing the Atlantic, and made a brief visit to Boston even though it had no playhouse. What hope of that at present?

Dan's parents insisted that he should not cut short his stay in England. '*You seem to be making progress,*' his father wrote. '*Do not throw it away now.*'

'He is very sensible,' said Jessica with relief.

'But . . . suppose it comes to a war?' Dan asked.

'How could it? A *war*? Your colony isn't a foreign country.'

Soon, though, Dan's fears were realised. News came, through the London papers, that General Gage's troops had been in action against the rebel colonists in Massachusetts.

'Lexington!' Dan exclaimed in horror. 'And Concord! I know both those places. They're only a few miles outside Boston!'

His father's next letter brought details not given in the newspapers. The redcoats had been soundly beaten. *'Ninety-three of ours were killed,'* he reported, *'and two hundred and seventy-three of the British.'*

'How terrible!' said Jessica. 'I can hardly believe it.'

But soon the London press were proclaiming a British victory at Bunker Hill. That too was just outside Boston. Dan had often walked over it as a boy. The name brought back vivid memories of the sea breeze and the birds, the city spread below, the blue Atlantic stretching out beyond.

'Our people fought hard,' wrote his father. *'They were only a scratch bunch of half-trained volunteers that Colonel Prescott had got together. It took the redcoats three attacks to take the hill – and again their losses were enormous.'*

Only two days earlier the various colonies had agreed on appointing a commander-in-chief. '*Of what?*' the letter went on gloomily. '*We have nothing you could call a proper army. But I gather that this George Washington is a fine man and an experienced commander – he fought against the French in the Canadian campaign. He is a Virginian, of course, a southerner, but perhaps that is a good thing. If we are to be forced into this deplorable conflict we shall need all the colonies to stand together, the south as well as the north.*'

'I don't know what to do,' said Dan. Were his brothers involved? Could he get back if he tried? Boston was still a closed port, except to troopships from England. Some of his father's vessels were still trading somewhere, having escaped being bottled up in their home port, but they were not venturing into British waters. His letters, forwarded by the reliable Mr Widdowson, travelled roundabout routes through various foreign traders.

Would the news of the fighting make him unpopular with his fellow-actors? He was, after all, born and bred in this notorious trouble spot, Boston. But they hardly seemed to connect him with such faraway events. He had been in England now for some time. He was liked. How could he be thought of as a 'rebel'? Anyhow, this dispute would soon blow over . . .

Only one member of the company did not show this easy-going indifference. Digby missed no chance to sneer or hint at Dan's possible disloyalty. But there was a quite different reason for that – jealousy. Dan was getting parts that would previously have been Digby's. And his close relations with Jessica, now obvious to all the company and good-humouredly accepted by them, were a humiliating reminder to Digby of his own failure in that field.

Apart from Digby's snide remarks, though, Dan was unaware of any hostility to him as an individual. But he could not blind himself to a general shift in public feeling. A year ago there had been more sympathy for the Americans – more argument in Parliament and in the newspapers. But armed rebellion, defiance of the King, the shooting of British soldiers . . . things were going too far.

One incident brought this home to him.

He was starting out from his lodgings one Sunday evening when, almost on the doorstep, he ran into David Garrick.

What was *he* doing here in this shabby byway off Fleet Street? 'Were you looking for me, sir?'

Dan stammered, and then could have bitten his tongue off for imagining that the mighty theatre manager would do such a thing, instead of sending a messenger. But Garrick laughed good-naturedly.

'No, Mr Carnaby. I am calling on one of your neighbours – the illustrious Dr Samuel Johnson.'

'Oh, of course. Yes, sir. That's his door.' Dan pointed.

'I know it well. I should!' Garrick smiled. 'Are you acquainted with him?'

'Oh, *no*, sir.' Dan had known the name since childhood days in Boston, where it was widely respected by cultured people. Johnson was known for his splendid edition of Shakespeare's plays and his famous English dictionary. Since lodging in Bolt Court, Dan had come to know the man by sight and been thrilled to think he was seeing such a celebrity in the flesh.

The doctor was an elderly, burly man, with an ugly mottled face, untidy in dress and uncouth in manner. One would see him stumping along Fleet Street with a massive stick, his empty hand tapping the wooden posts that lined the footway. He seemed to have a superstition about those posts, for once or twice Dan had seen him turn back, with an impatient exclamation, and then start off again, touching each post with great deliberation. He must be superstitious, thought Dan. Imagines it'll be bad luck to miss one.

'You must meet him,' said Garrick. 'Something to remember!'

'It would be an honour, sir.'

The door was opened to them by another man he had often seen passing to and fro: a well-dressed, middle-aged West Indian, who was generally supposed to be Dr Johnson's manservant.

Garrick greeted him cordially. 'The Doctor's expecting me, Mr Barber—'

'Yes, indeed, Mr Garrick!'

'And I want to present this young gentleman to him – Mr Carnaby, from the theatre.'

Mr Barber led the way upstairs.

Johnson treated Mr Barber almost as an adopted son. It was an interesting story. The man had been born in Jamaica, given his freedom as a child, brought to England by his former master and sent to school in Yorkshire. When his master died, Johnson was asked to give him a home. Johnson had just lost his wife, had no children himself, and could never resist such an appeal. He had paid for the rest of Frank Barber's education and been like a father to him ever afterwards. Now with an English wife and three children, he was back under the Doctor's roof.

Johnson, Garrick assured Dan, was the most kind-hearted of men. Over the years, he had collected a variety of unfortunates in his over-large house. They nearly drove him mad with their quarrels, but he never turned them out.

Johnson might love his fellow-men but he also loved an argument. That was obvious when they entered the upstairs room. The Doctor, an imposing figure, stood in a ring of half a dozen gentlemen, laying down the law and flattening any opposition. Dan realised with dismay that they were discussing America.

Their arrival caused a brief interruption. Garrick was warmly greeted and presented Dan. 'Some of you may be familiar with his admirable work in the theatre.'

There was a polite but unconvincing murmur. Johnson smiled kindly, but could not lie. 'I fear I seldom go to the play, nowadays.'

'You saw him when I revived *She Stoops to Conquer*,' Garrick reminded him.

'Ah, poor Goldsmith! A splendid playwright!' the Doctor recalled sadly.

'He wrote like an angel,' Garrick admitted,

'though he talked like poor Poll.'

From the laughter Dan guessed that Goldsmith's everyday conversation had not matched the wit of his dialogue.

'I should explain,' Garrick went on, 'that Mr Carnaby comes from the country you were discussing. I am confident you will make him no less welcome?'

'No man can choose where he is born,' said the Doctor. He thrust out a massive paw and honoured Dan with a warm handshake. 'Perhaps he can answer some of the questions that perplex us?' Dan braced himself, wishing that he were older and better qualified to face a cross-examination.

'For instance!' The speaker was youngish, very elegant in dress, almost a man-about-town, Scottish by his voice. 'Your leaders complain a great deal about their lack of freedom. Is not this hypocrisy, when in your own country you have slaves everywhere?'

Dan choked back the indignant answer that sprang to his lips. 'There are no slaves, sir, where *I* come from—'

'And exactly where do you come from?'

'Boston, sir. Massachusetts.' Dan said it with pride.

'Boston? The very centre of all this agitation!'

'But not of slavery, sir. The slaves are in the southern colonies, where the plantations are. In the north there's a great feeling against slavery. I believe it started in Pennsylvania, because it was the Quakers who founded that colony—'

'Quakers!' The Scottish voice was full of contempt. Those idealistic folk were not so highly respected as they were on the other side of the Atlantic.

But the Doctor said, 'I do not share all their views, Boswell, but they have campaigned well against slavery in our own country. You've been given a fair enough answer.'

He took control of the argument. Dan prepared himself grimly to be demolished. The Doctor was what people over here called a 'a real old Tory', resolute in support of the King and his government. If the English paid tax on all the tea they drank, why shouldn't the colonies? Dan hoped he would not ask questions about the Boston Tea Party.

'We just fought an expensive war against France, and we are still paying for it! Where would you have been if we had not sent an army to take Quebec? Paying taxes to the King of France instead of King George!'

Dan thought it best not to argue such points. He knew that nobody at home still worried about the French. The redcoats were not sent over now to defend them from French invasion, but to keep them in subjection to London. Nor were they needed for protection if the Indians came on the warpath. The settlers, dead-shots with their rifles, were quite capable of that.

At last Dr Johnson seemed to remember that he had other guests. He gave up his harangue, asked a few good-tempered questions, and turned away. Dan could not help overhearing the Scotsman's disparaging comment about 'impudent young dogs' – or the Doctor's almost indignant retort.

'But, my dear Boswell, I love the acquaintance of these young people! I don't like to think myself growing old. Young men have more virtue than old men. They have more generous sentiments. I *love* the "young dogs" of this age.'

In that crowded room, with so much talk going on at the same time, one could not help catching remarks not intended for one's own ears.

The frank comments about Americans did not worry Dan too much. They were a necessary reminder that this more critical attitude was developing. English soldiers were dying and being buried in American soil. He could not always expect the friendly welcome he had met when he'd first arrived.

It was quite a different kind of remark, however, that left a new and darker cloud on his horizon at the end of the evening.

A man behind him was talking earnestly to Garrick. 'I could not believe it! Drury Lane will not be the same. Your retirement, after all these years—'

An urgent whisper cut him short. 'Hush! There must be no announcement for a few days.'

'I am sorry, Mr Garrick—'

So was Dan, as the significance dawned upon him. Garrick was giving up. How would this affect his own future – and Jessica's? Indeed, everybody's?

He must get away from here. He might have outstayed his welcome anyhow. He threaded his way through the crowd and stood until, without interrupting anybody, he could take courteous leave of his host. An unforgettable evening, he could say in all sincerity . . . though with one memory, he thought, that he only wished he could forget.

At the door he came face to face with Garrick. He thanked him. The manager kept hold of his hand, looking into Dan's face with an anxious smile.

'I fear that just now you may have overheard something you were not meant to?'

'Well, sir—' What could he say?

'Never fear,' Garrick whispered. 'All will be well. But for the moment I must ask you not to breathe a word to anybody. You understand? *Anybody*.'

'Of course. I promise.'

That was the worst thing. For the first time there was a secret he could not share with Jessica.

Fourteen

The strain did not last long, for the news broke a few days later. Mr Garrick had sold out to Mr Richard Brinsley Sheridan, the brilliant young playwright whose comedy *The Rivals* had been such a triumphant success last year at Covent Garden. Garrick had done his best to make sure that none of his faithful team should suffer from this change in management.

Jessica – little knowing the anxiety Dan had suffered for the past week – was greatly excited. After all, dear Mr Garrick had given his whole life to Drury Lane, he had been acting less and less himself lately, he had surely earned a happy retirement with his delightful wife in their riverside home. Mr Sheridan, on the other hand, was only twenty-four, handsome, charming and as brilliantly witty as the plays he was said to dash off with such incredible speed. Garrick, of course, was something of a writer too – he had written poetry and plays of his own, as well as adapting and revising other people's – but he had not Sheridan's genius. Audiences would be rocking with laughter at Sheridan's comedies after another two hundred years, when Garrick's were all forgotten.

She looked forward to working under such an interesting young man. But first there would be Garrick's farewell season.

He planned to revive the plays in which he had first made his name all those years ago. Richard III, Hamlet, Macbeth, King Lear – he brought the same dynamic energy to those parts that he had shown as a young man. He played Benedick in *Much Ado*, to show that he was no less a master of comedy. Veteran theatre-goers declared that it was a miracle; just what they remembered from so long ago. Why was this man retiring?

For Jessica and Dan it was especially wonderful. They were seeing these legendary performances they could never have hoped to see, simply because they had been born too late. Time had rolled back to make the miracle.

Dan had been learning everything he could since his first arrival in Bath. Mind and memory were packed. So was a notebook, with scribbled technical details, titles, names. All might be needed when he got home, if he was to fulfil his American playhouse dream.

Garrick's farewell season was not confined to

the Shakespearean plays for which he had done so much. He ended with an old comedy, *The Wonder, a Woman Keeps a Secret*. He clearly enjoyed his original part of Don Felix, a lively character.

'By Susannah Centlivre?' Dan read from the playbill. 'A woman!'

'And why not?' demanded Jessica.

'Soon after Nell Gwyn's time,' said the learned Mr Dodd. 'She favoured breeches parts. Like you. They say she was rather mannish in appearance. Not like you.'

'Thank God,' said Jessica.

Dan checked the impulse to say 'Amen'.

So, on 10 June, David Garrick's long management of Drury Lane ended. And in less than a month something else happened that was to have an even greater effect upon their lives.

'*On the fourth of July, at Philadelphia,*' wrote Dan's father, '*all the colonies combined to sign a Declaration of Independence. They are now the Thirteen United States of America.*' They had finally thrown off their allegiance to the English king. Some of the phrasing was rather fine, he considered. '*We hold these truths to be self-evident, that all men are created equal . . .*' And '*Life, Liberty, and the Pursuit of Happiness . . .*' No doubt the learned Dr Johnson could argue eloquently against it, but he would not convert many people in Boston.

Especially now. Washington had forced the redcoats to leave the city. He had simply massed all his cannon on the high ground overlooking it until General Gage knew that his position was hopeless. He withdrew his forces. '*Never to come back, I hope,*' forecast Mr Carnaby – rightly, as things turned out. Boston was a free port again. Ships could come in and out, provided they did not run into a British naval vessel. Carnaby's was getting its business back to normal: '*We are getting much sympathy – and co-operation from the French and Dutch.*'

Dan felt vastly relieved. So often his conscience had nagged him. Should he be here – in London, of all places – when the folks at home were undergoing such difficulties?

Jessica had done her best to comfort him: 'Even if you had gone back, what could you have *done*? You are not a soldier.' She had the English idea of soldiering. It was all right for a few gentlemen to swagger about in splendid uniforms, holding the King's commission, but it was not an occupation that ordinary young men considered. It was for low-class, unskilled illiterates, often with criminal records. Her ideas were drawn from the stage, from comedies like *The Recruiting Officer* and scallywags like those Falstaff had commanded.

'Have you met any young man in London', she demanded, 'who feels guilty because he's not going over to fight for the king he swears he's loyal to?'

Dan had no answer to that. It was common talk that the government was having to recruit the troops it needed by hiring mercenaries from the King's possessions in Germany.

He turned with relief to what concerned him more urgently: strengthening his position under the new management.

On the whole Sheridan had kept his promise to Garrick, that members of the company should not suffer from the change. The only notable exception was poor young Sarah Siddons. She and her husband soon got notice that their services were no longer required.

There was sympathy in the company, but not much surprise. A husband like hers, of second-rate acting quality, would be a handicap to anyone. 'And she herself was too often miscast,' said Jessica. 'Comedy is not her strong point. She might be wonderful in tragedy – if she gets the chance.'

'I agree,' said Dan. 'I think one day she'll be back here.'

No one else suffered in the changeover. Even Digby kept his place, though he had been going through a bad spell. Some whispered that the young man was going to the dogs. He was drinking more than he should. Others said that he was drinking too much because, more and more, Mr Carnaby was getting parts he thought should have been his. He was spending too much time at Vauxhall and other places of pleasure. He had picked up an infection there – it often happened – and had been off work completely for a short time.

Dan saw little of him, though they still lodged in the same house. Digby posed as a great patriot, stinging Dan with sneers about Americans. It was better to keep out of his way.

Especially when autumn brought news that Sir William Howe had taken Rhode Island and occupied New York. Digby, backstage, was boasting to everyone how the theatre in John Street – the one that had first inspired Dan – had added 'Royal' to its name and was full every night of the victorious redcoats. It was some consolation when Washington crossed the Delaware river and defeated the imported Hessians.

Most of the company, however, were fully

absorbed in their first season under Sheridan. He put on *Romeo and Juliet*, but Jessica's hopes were dashed when the title role went to her wild young rival, Mary Robinson. He revived several of Congreve's old comedies, altering many of the ruder bits that might offend a proper-minded audience. He did the same with Vanbrugh's *The Relapse*, with even more cuts and alterations, adding songs and music, and renaming it *A Trip to Scarborough*. At one point an actress was hissed off the stage. Jessica and Dan were lucky enough not to suffer such treatment.

There was general relief when they heard that their new manager was writing a new comedy which would outdo *The Rivals* in brilliance and form a climax when the season closed in May.

But would it be ready in time? Sheridan was known as a fast worker, his pen covered the paper at unbelievable speed. But it was now realised that a finished script did not pour from it. 'They say Shakespeare never blotted out a line,' said Mr Dodd anxiously, 'but I wish that this young man was the same. It's all cut, cut, rephrase, rephrase.'

Everybody was getting anxious when they heard that *School for Scandal* had been handed over to the copyist. Someone who had caught a glimpse of it said that under the curtain-line was scribbled, '*Finished at last, thank God, R. B. Sheridan*'. The prompter had added, '*Amen, W. Hopkins*'. Everyone echoed that.

Now they had to master their impatience until the play could be read aloud to the whole company. And cast. Everyone wanted to be in it. Some would be disappointed.

To Dan, sharing the general anxiety, another cheerful letter from home brought a welcome break. Boston was getting back to normal. The war dragged on in other parts, both sides claimed successes, but there was a growing belief that the English would tire first. Washington had performed wonders, turning his untrained material into a disciplined army. '*We hear there is much sympathy for us in Europe*', wrote Mr Carnaby. '*Especially in France. It seems that a young French captain of dragoons, the Marquis de la Fayette, is enlisting volunteers to fight on our side. Perhaps France might become our ally. Do you know anything about this? We should be glad of any information. Now that you are meeting some of these important people in London.*'

Dan's family had been impressed by his recollections of that evening at Dr Johnson's. Had he exaggerated a little and given them the wrong idea? Dr Johnson's friends were 'important' only in the literary sense; they were not in Parliament or the government.

Dan smiled at the thought that by living in London he gained any inside knowledge. The war news seldom cropped up in the dressing-room at Drury Lane, unless something sensational happened. Like, just recently, the case of the British spy. Curiously, his father's letter did not mention that.

An Englishman, serving in the army there, had been caught spying, then been tried and sentenced to death. Fair enough, it was agreed by the dressing-room. What outraged everyone was that the unfortunate fellow had been hanged, when they all knew he was an officer and a gentleman. 'What *should* they have done?' Jessica asked, when the debate reached the ears of the ladies. 'Shot him, of course,' Mr Smith assured her. 'Blindfolded, with a proper firing squad! A death with dignity.' Jessica could not see what difference it made; rope or bullet, they killed the poor man. Gentleman Smith snorted. How could you expect a young woman to appreciate such points? 'If our people catch an American spying, after this, Heaven help him.'

Interest in this news item was quickly overlaid

by the first reading to the company of Sheridan's comedy.

From the opening lines – Lady Sneerwell at her dressing-table, plotting mischief with the odious Mr Snake as he sipped his drinking chocolate – there was incessant and hilarious laughter. There was no doubt, from the word go, that their new manager had come up with a success. Some characters were created to fit particular members. Their casting was almost inevitable. Old friends exchanged delighted smiles. A lip-reader could have interpreted the silent congratulations and good wishes: 'You to a T, darling! Best of luck!' Other faces seemed to reflect quite other emotions. But the play itself was a winner, no doubt of that. The only worry, for some, was, would they be in it?

The piece was a satire on fashionable London society, of which the author had a wide experience. The heroine was a wealthy and beautiful young orphan, Maria, ward of comical old Sir Peter Teazle. A perfect part for Jessica, thought Dan, but more likely to fall to Mary Robinson, who had the looks for these ingénue roles but (in her own life) none of the purity and innocence assumed in the plot. But Garrick was coming back to produce this play, and as

Mary had originally been his own discovery he would almost certainly select her.

The handsome young hero, loving Maria not for her money but for herself, was the good-natured spendthrift Charles Surface. Just the part for Gentleman Smith. But he would be constantly outwitted by his unscrupulous brother, Joseph, who would pretend devotion to the girl but really be after nothing but her fortune. All kinds of tricks, disguises and deceptions carried the story forward, scene after scene. Many of the characters had appropriate names: Sir Toby Bumper and Sir Benjamin Backbite, Careless and Crabtree and Mrs Candour.

That last part was given to Jane Pope, who was generally agreed to be excellent in it. To Jessica, this was immensely encouraging, for it proved that an actress who grew out of breeches parts could go on to a triumphant second career.

The immediate, nail-biting question for the two friends would be how they fared in all this intense competition.

Jessica was first to learn her fate. She was summoned to the manager's room where Garrick sat closeted with Sheridan. The younger man pulled up another chair for her. He came quickly to the point. 'We are agreed, Mrs Stone, we should like you – if you are willing – to play Maria.'

Willing? She could not suppress a little gasp of relief. 'I – thought—'

Sheridan smiled. 'And what did you think?'

'People were saying – most of us supposed – Mrs Robinson—' This was too good to be true.

'I originally considered Mrs Robinson. But I learn that by the time the play goes on she will not, er, look the part.'

'She finds that she is going to have a child,' said Garrick disapprovingly. 'She says it will unshape her.'

So Mary's notorious goings-on had at last caught up with her. It was not for Jessica to comment. She was bursting to tell Dan what was, for herself, such a fortunate consequence. So, when his own summons came to the manager's room an hour or two later, he was still full of her happiness, though braced for disappointment himself.

His heart sank at the playwright's apologetic tone. 'Ah, Mr Carnaby! It's been difficult working in everybody. But I've done my best. You have an excellent singing voice. I need someone good for that drinking-song in the third act.'

Dan remembered it. A good song, with a catchy tune.

163

   'Here's to the maiden of bashful fifteen,
   Here's to the widow of fifty—'

And a rousing chorus:

   'Let the toast pass –
   Drink to the lass –
   I'll warrant she'll prove an excuse for a glass.'

He remembered too how tiny the part was for the man who sang it.

Sheridan read his thoughts. 'A small part, I fear. But we have something else important for you, even if it's only an understudy.' This did little to raise Dan's spirits. Until Sheridan went on. 'But it's for Gentleman Smith. You know about his Monday evenings? He won't give them up. The end of *our* season coincides with the end of the stag-hunting. There will be at least two Mondays when you have to take over the Charles Surface part.'

Dan's spirits rose. A leading role. And playing opposite Jessica! Two nights anyhow. A real chance to prove his quality. 'What about my song, those nights?' he asked.

'You can still sing it – but as Charles Surface. He's on in that scene,' said Sheridan. 'And those few lines you have as Sir Toby? Oh, the nights you're Charles Surface they can be spoken by Mr Digby. He's on as Second Gentleman. He'll be glad to take them over.'

Dan wondered . . .

Fifteen

It was good to be working with Garrick again. He had emerged briefly from retirement to help his successor in his early difficulties.

Dan and Jessica liked Sheridan and his beautiful wife Elizabeth well enough – there was only a few years' gap between the couples – but Dick Sheridan was not so completely a man of the theatre as Garrick was. A genius as a playwright, admittedly, but he was distracted by quite different ambitions: to get into Parliament, to make his way in wealthy and titled society. Knocking off witty masterpieces was just a means to make the money needed.

To Garrick the theatre was everything. Costume, candlelight, characterisation . . . His active mind was eager for new ideas about everything in the craft. Dan was constantly learning and noting details for future use.

Understudying Gentleman Smith was a valuable experience. He learnt not only from Garrick's conception of the part but from Mr Smith's too. He was another man from whom much could be learnt, and one day adapted to other parts in other plays. If there was one drawback it was that Dan could contribute really nothing of his own. He was an understudy. If, once in a while, he would have preferred to do something differently, he must suppress the urge. On nights when he took over the part he must not present Jessica and the rest of the cast with an altered Charles Surface. He must reproduce Gentleman Smith's exact moves, tone and timing. It did not worry him. He did not often imagine that his own idea was better.

The spring days went happily by. He and Jessica discussed the coming months when Drury Lane would be closed. Should they try to join a touring company? Or seek short-term engagements at the other London playhouses, which were freer to fill the gap when the royal theatres took their break? With their improving pay they had less need now to worry about money.

'And there is another thing,' said Jessica hesitantly. 'It is a long time since I saw my mother...' She paused and looked at him. 'It can be difficult – if you are acting, you can't come and go at will. I should like to see her.'

'And so should I!'

'I'm so glad to hear you say that.'

'Well, if you haven't changed your mind. About *me*.'

'Do you think I could?'

'Then you had better present me to her. Things seem to be going well. Not just here in the theatre. But in America.'

'You think this awful war is going to end?'

'Yes. And the colonies – the states, I mean – are going to win. The English will tire first. And if France comes in as America's ally—'

It seemed increasingly probable. Would Britain want another war with her ancient enemy? Fighting in two continents?

Things might happen quickly. If they did, new possibilities may offer themselves with startling suddenness. And with both their careers making their present progress—

'Oh, Dan – I hardly dare to hope—'

'We might not have to wait any longer. There could be that little ceremony in Boston . . . It would be a good idea if I went with you, to see your mother, before too long.'

They postponed further discussion until after the first night of *School for Scandal*.

That went well. The theatre shook with almost continuous laughter as one neat line followed another. The moment Garrick had foretold would make a triumphant climax – when Lady Teazle was disclosed crouching behind a screen – almost stopped the performance with its seemingly endless roll of applause. Watching it, Dan longed for the first Monday evening when he, not Gentleman Smith, would be Charles Surface, the one to snatch aside the screen and cry, 'Lady Teazle by all that's wonderful!' To which her scandalised husband would answer, 'Lady Teazle, by all that's damnable!'

That first night he could only claim his own tiny share of the credit for an unforgettable performance. Yet the audience were so warmed up by the total effect that even his rendering of the drinking song was rapturously encored:

'Let the toast pass –
Drink to the lass –
I'll warrant she'll prove an excuse for a glass.'

Jessica's portrayal of the lovely heroine would have proved an excuse for any number of glasses.

It figured prominently in the press reviews. The *Morning Post* was especially favourable. Mr Bate had not forgotten that Mrs Stone was his own discovery. And a few days later, after Dan's first appearance as Gentleman's Smith's understudy, he slipped in a note to that effect. '*Henceforth,*' he wrote, '*Daniel Carnaby will be a young actor to keep our eyes on.*'

Gentleman Smith's devotion to sport proved most fortunate for Dan. On the second Monday he took a fence too recklessly, had a fall, and acquired an ungainly limp which made it temporarily impossible to swagger on as an elegant man-about-town.

'So I'm afraid, Mr Carnaby,' said Sheridan apologetically, 'you will just have to carry on.'

There seemed for once – so far as Dan and Jessica could selfishly observe – not a cloud on the horizon.

But the next day, entering the almost deserted dressing-room, he recognised the back view of Gilbert Digby. He stopped instinctively and stepped back, not fancying a disagreeable solo encounter, but then he realised they were not completely alone. In his unmistakable voice, Mr Dodd was saying rather severely, 'I would advise you not to repeat remarks like that, young man.'

'Why not? If they are true?'

'But *are* they? Have you evidence?' Digby's mumbled answer was inaudible. Both actors had their backs to the door. 'Some young men,' Dodd went on, 'would think allegations like that justified a challenge to a duel. He is an American, certainly, but that does not mean he is a traitor.'

At this point Dan stepped backwards, quite silently, from the room. He wished he had done so earlier. Digby, out of malice, must have been talking the most utter nonsense. It would be unwise to overhear another word. As Dodd said, some people might feel that such slanders must be challenged. Literally 'challenged'. With swords or pistols. He did not want to get mixed up in anything like that.

Later, confiding in Jessica, he made light of the incident and was surprised when *she* did not.

'I've been wondering whether I should tell you,' she said in a worried tone. 'But at the time I thought, as you seem to, that it was better to ignore it. I didn't want to alarm you.'

'I'm not alarmed. It's so silly. I'm not a spy. I've done nothing to suggest I am. How could I – here?'

The British government still claimed that Americans were subjects of King George. They could not be regarded as 'enemies' or 'rebels' until they acted as such. Even Boston was still full of people who did not ask for Independence – people who were openly planning to move to Canada if the colonies became 'the United States'. His father had told him—

'Ah, those letters from your father! Have you kept them?'

'Of course! Why ever not?'

'Could there be anything in them? That people could twist?'

He laughed at her fears. But that evening, half an hour after getting back to his lodgings, he was beckoned by his landlord. 'Have you seen Mr Digby?'

'No. Why?'

'I think he was wanting a word. He was asking if you were back. I said I didn't know. He went up, looking for you. He still hasn't seen you?'

'No. If he wants me—' Dan shrugged indifferently.

Later that night he ran into Digby, who passed him without a word. Well, if he doesn't want me, thought Dan, I certainly don't want *him*.

Next morning a thought suddenly struck him. He opened the drawer in which he kept, carefully folded, his letters from home. The drawer was empty.

Sixteen

His fears had been well founded.

They had been there yesterday morning. He could not believe the servant-girl would have taken them. Digby had been asking Mr Blagg if Dan was in – apparently to make certain that he was *not*. He had seen Dan later, but had said nothing. Blagg remembered that Digby had gone upstairs after his first inquiry. That must have been when he removed the letters.

But why? Why on earth?

There was nothing secret in them. They were ordinary family letters, mainly from his father but often with loving postscripts from his mother. If Digby had been hoping for the 'evidence' that Mr Dodd had challenged him to produce – proof that Dan was an American spy – he must have been sadly disappointed when he read through them at leisure. Perhaps, when Dan came back, he would find the papers restored to their usual place. Digby would suppose Dan had never noticed that they were missing.

In any case, he could scarcely storm downstairs and accuse Digby. He could imagine Mr Dodd's disapproving question, addressed this time to himself. 'Where is your evidence?' If Digby was capable of stealing from a colleague's bedroom he would not be such a fool as to keep the stolen items in his own. If Digby had quickly realised how useless those letters were for his purpose, they were probably now torn up into small scraps and floating down the Thames to the sea.

There was no point in making a fuss or asking offensive questions. The letters were harmless. He was merely angry at Digby's unforgivable behaviour, and sorry to have lost them.

'Are you quite sure they're harmless?' Jessica asked, when he confided in her later that day. She seemed more worried than he was.

'Of course!' he exclaimed, almost angrily. 'I let you read them yourself.'

He had often done so, as they had grown closer in recent months. She loved hearing about his family, longed for the day when she would meet them all, and eventually be taken into their circle. Those letters offered the only way at present of getting to know them.

'I just wondered, thinking back,' she said

apologetically, 'there were sometimes bits that were a shade ambiguous.'

'*Ambiguous*?'

'They could be understood in some other way – quite by accident. If a malicious person wanted to twist your father's perfectly innocent phrasing—'

He thought back. It was easier for him. She had heard or read the letters only once. He himself – he was not ashamed to admit to her – had read and reread some of them a number of times. 'My remedy for homesickness,' he'd confessed to her with an embarrassed laugh. 'Why not?' she said. She was an understanding girl.

So he was better placed than she was to recall the precise wording that someone like Digby could pick out and interpret in a different sense. '*Now that you are meeting some of these important people in London . . . We should be glad of any information . . . We hear there is much sympathy for us in Europe.*' Though the respectable Carnabys had never thought of themselves as rebels, Dan's father had shown clearly how, month by month, he had become increasingly indignant at the line taken by King George and his ministers.

If Digby's mind had become so warped by jealousy he might actually turn informer and go to the authorities. Since the British public's sense of outrage at the hanging of that officer for spying, the government would jump at any chance to mete out similar treatment to an American. Dan began to realise that his father's letters might not be quite as harmless as he had imagined. But he tried to reassure Jessica.

'Surely the rest of the sheet would have made Father's real meaning plain? Digby can't just take scissors and cut out the sentence or two that back up his story.'

'No. But he need not tell them that he was able to steal the whole sheet. He could easily pretend it would have given him away. Say, he had to leave most of the papers where they were. Just sneaking odd pages here and there to support his story.'

'You think they'd believe him?'

'I think these high-up people will sometimes believe anything they *want* to believe. Digby himself would. What they want at this moment is an American spy they can hang.' Her voice faltered over that last word. 'Oh, Dan – you must realise – you may be in real danger.'

'Possibly. But only possibly.'

'Digby hates you. He's been spreading these stories about you. I think he'd do anything.'

'But what more *has* he done? Sneak into my room. Take away some private letters. Not the conduct of a gentleman! But we don't know what he'll do with them. If anything.'

The season had still a week to run. Dan could not imagine Digby making any move to cause an upset in those final days. It would certainly not improve the fellow's popularity with Mr Sheridan. And that was where Digby's own ambitions lay.

'Not to mention yours and mine,' said Dan. He would not for a moment consider making some excuse, throwing up that splendid role as Charles Surface, and getting out of London.

They had not yet made any firm commitment for the next few weeks. It might be a good time to pay that visit to Jessica's mother in the Cotswold Hills. And a good place to go to, far from London and any government inquiries about him.

Jessica agreed. And apologised for becoming so nervous. They must enjoy this closing week at Drury Lane to the full. 'Full' was the word for the theatre, too. Night after night after night.

Two days later the tension came back. As Dan entered the theatre he caught the eye of the old boxkeeper, Johnston. Johnston's eye could beckon like anyone else's forefinger. Dan went over, pausing to stroke the man's immense watchdog.

The two had built up a wordless friendship. If the dog took to anyone, Johnston regarded it as a testimonial of character.

'A word in your ear, Mr Carnaby!'

'At your service.'

'I name no names. You know somebody has been spreading ridiculous rumours.'

'Indeed?' Dan stiffened, instantly on guard.

'About American spies – in London! This person has been going round the taverns hereabouts. My son-in-law met him. Very confident, he seemed. Swearing the government is on to something. Ready to bet there'll be someone arrested within the week.'

'He does sound sure.'

'He's not offered to bet with anyone here.'

'You surprise me.' They both knew it was Digby they were discussing.

'My son-in-law reckons the young man must have inside knowledge. He's trying to bet on a certainty; not quite the thing a real gentleman should do. I've asked my son-in-law to lay a bet with him on my behalf . . . not mentioning my name.'

'So – in spite of his inside knowledge – you're risking a bet that no one *will* be arrested?'

The old man chuckled. 'I don't mind betting

on a certainty. But then I'm no true gentleman.'

'I hope you win,' said Dan, with feeling.

Johnston smiled and looked confident. He had dropped his hint and believed in Dan. Dan felt less sure. What could he do to make sure Johnston did not lose his money?

Plans were back in the melting-pot. It was clear that Digby had now taken some definite action. He must have been to a person in authority – a magistrate or perhaps someone in government circles – and reported his suspicions that his American colleague was a spy, collecting information in London to send over to the rebels. He must have made a good enough case for action to be promised.

'Arrested within the week,' Digby had said. The cunning beast must have given the authorities some reason for holding their hand for a day or two. He would not want the blame for a scandal that would mar the ending of the season.

Dan was reluctant to upset Jessica by telling her of the serious turn events were now taking. But he could not avoid it and, as he had feared, she implored him to slip out of London without wasting another day.

'Disappear? How can I?' he demanded. 'We are all right for these last few days. I feel certain. If

I walked out now, who would ever employ me again? Who could take over the part of Charles Surface? I *was* the understudy. Smith couldn't come back with his injured leg.'

'I can't stand much more of this,' she almost wailed. 'Don't you realise what could happen to you?'

He did. All too well. If this government laid hands on him there was little chance of a fair trial. It would give them a golden opportunity to regain popularity with their indignant public. Once they got him into a dock in court he might finish in a hangman's noose at Tyburn.

'Digby has worded his bet very carefully,' he told her. 'Within a week, he says. That leaves ample time after the theatre closes. And ample time for me to get away – without upsetting any*one* or any*thing*. You are going to enjoy the triumph of that last night! So am I, for that matter.' He forced himself to laugh. 'I'm an actor, too – haven't you realised how conceited and self-centred I can be?'

He promised that once the final curtain fell he would concentrate on his own safety. When a season ended people were apt to disperse in different directions. There was nothing suspicious about it.

'But if there is a warrant for your arrest—!'

'They can't serve it on me if they don't know where I've gone.'

'You need somewhere to hide.'

That was not so easy. Any Englishman – even a notorious highwayman – would have friends to shelter him. Where could Dan go? To the respectable Widdowsons in Bristol? Hardly, once they realised he was a fugitive from the law. Where else had he any friends? In Bath? He knew too many people in Bath, or rather too many in Bath knew him. After all that time acting, week after week, his reappearance in the city would be quickly noticed and talked about. But wherever he went, even to a district where he had never set foot before, he would be recognised as an American and suspected at a time like this.

'Perhaps this is the time to take you to see my mother?' Jessica suggested.

'I wouldn't risk landing her in possible trouble on my account. And I fancy – from what you've told me about your stepfather – that *he* would not exactly welcome a young stranger from America! He might ask awkward questions.'

Jessica saw the force of that. And the very loneliness of that farm in the hills might focus interest on the arrival of a colonial.

Dan decided reluctantly that, with the present war raging, England would not be the easiest country to hide in. 'It would be more sensible', he suggested, 'if I slipped across the Channel for a few weeks. Then, if nothing happens, if Digby's plan misfires and I know it's safe to come back . . . I *want* to see Paris. Garrick always says I should. There are things to be learnt there, things about the theatre.'

'But . . . can you get there?'

'Things can be arranged. I've worked in shipping. I remember the names of people my father had dealings with.'

The next day he was able to tell her, in quiet triumph, that he had arranged a passage – to Holland, actually – in a vessel now docked below London Bridge. It would sail on the early morning tide only a few hours after the curtain fell for the last time on *School for Scandal.*

'Couldn't be more convenient!' he said.

Jessica was much relieved, though dismayed at the thought of their parting.

'It's not forever,' he emphasised.

'I hope to God it isn't.'

'This war won't last much longer. How can it?'

It was fortunate they did not know that the

dingdong struggle, with alternating victories for both sides, would continue for a long time yet. They had a desperate faith that they were separating only for a few months at most.

They talked of what they should do on their last evening. They would have supper together after the final curtain.

'Let's go to the Devil,' Jessica suggested.

They both laughed. The Devil was an excellent tavern near Temple Bar, not far from Dan's lodgings. They had been there before. It was a very respectable establishment, where a well-dressed young lady could be taken by a gentleman without any sly glances or raised eyebrows. It was thought quite proper if they ate their meal in a private room.

That night, though, in view of the lateness of the hour, Jessica planned to dress as if for a breeches part. If strangers took them for a couple of young gentlemen, so much the better. She would feel less conspicuous. Dan willingly agreed.

'It'll be how we first met,' he reminded her. 'And it'll be nice to remember you—' He paused and hastily added, 'Though it's not going to be long.' She was not the weeping sort, but she looked not far from tears.

The evening came. Dan had slipped down to London Bridge in the morning, carefully avoiding Digby lest his light baggage be noticed. He stowed it aboard the Dutch vessel, explained that he would be returning late in the evening, long before they sailed on the early morning tide.

The theatre was already packed when he arrived. Old Johnston said every box was taken. Dan bent over to stroke the dog. 'Don't forget me, Bear,' he whispered softly. The great beast licked his hand.

That evening was a fashionable occasion. Mrs Sheridan, who helped her husband on the business side by keeping very accurate accounts, had assured them that the play had taken more money at every performance than any piece that season. Behind the scenes there was a light-hearted, excitable atmosphere that reminded Dan of breaking-up day at school. He found it hard to get into that spirit himself (there were too many more serious thoughts at the back of his mind), but as the performance went on he began to share the general mood. The actor in him took charge. (In later years Jessica would remind him that he had acted with genius. 'I knew from then on,' she recalled, 'that you would end up as a king of comedy.')

He was thinking of her when he sang, for the last time:

'Let the toast pass –
Drink to the lass –
I'll warrant she'll prove an excuse for a glass.'

He brought the house down when he snatched aside the screen to disclose Lady Teazle's hiding-place and cried out, 'Lady Teazle, by all that's wonderful!' And, in the closing speech of the play, broke into verse to promise Jessica, as heroine:

'Though thou, dear maid, shouldst waive thy beauty's sway,
Thou still must rule, because I will obey!'

He finished his speech – and the play. The curtain came down in a tumult of applause. It rose again, as Mrs Abington (who, being leading lady, had played Lady Teazle) sailed forward to deliver the rhymed epilogue. Another ovation for her. Then it was curtain up and curtain down constantly, with more and more clapping. At last, with relief, Dan could escape to the dressing-room.

Mechanically he exchanged compliments and

congratulations with the other men as they struggled out of their costumes. There was only one person in the world he wanted to talk to. The precious minutes were rushing by.

Would he ever see this room again – or even these people? Would Digby's scheming turn out to be a failure, a false alarm, a horrible nightmare without reality?

Would he be back again in this theatre, building on the success of the past few days, only a few months from now?

He pulled on his shoes. He would get out now with the least possible exchange of words. He must parry questions (but pleasantly); reveal nothing that might be repeated.

He had arranged with Jessica that he would wait for her in the shadows outside the stage door. Much better that they should not be seen leaving together. She would get too many questions fired at her anyhow.

The door-keeper's little lobby was crowded. He started to edge his way out. Suddenly came Digby's voice, loud and clear. 'This is your man, my friends!' A massive chest rose like a wall in front of him. There was a gush of hot beer-laden breath in his face as a portentous voice addressed him: 'Daniel Carnaby, in the King's name, I arrest you as a spy!'

'*And* a dirty rebel—' Digby began to add, before Dan's fist crashed on to his jaw.

Seventeen

Dan felt an agonising pain as his arms were gripped from behind and he was jerked swiftly backwards. The second constable was as tall as the first, if not so burly. Both, when he had a chance to see them properly, looked like old soldiers, grizzled maybe, but still muscular and well-versed in exercising their strength. For a moment he struggled, but gave up as he felt the ruthless twist of his right arm.

'Resisting arrest,' cried the first man delightedly. 'Assault too, if this gentleman cares to bring a charge.' He snatched up the door-keeper's pen. 'Better get some names of witnesses.'

This provoked instant hubbub. Most of the actors seemed reluctant to offer their names. Whether this was due to sympathy with Dan, or because they genuinely planned to be out of town and did not want to be delayed by court proceedings, he had no means of telling.

Someone said, 'I think we should send for Mr Sheridan,' but another voice answered, 'We had better not! Remember, he is entertaining His

Royal Highness.' The Prince of Wales and his friends had honoured this last night with their presence. The manager would be furious if such an occasion was marred by an incident of this sort.

'You can tell Mr Sheridan later,' said the constable. 'Let me get this scoundrel under lock and key.' He scribbled down a few names and nodded to his companion.

They left, shoving Dan before them, the second constable maintaining that iron grip on Dan's arm. At the least sign of resistance came an awful twist. Dan gave up the attempt.

It was not far to Bow Street, where they told him he would spend the night in the lock-up. He would go before the magistrate first thing in the morning. He knew that any attempt to break loose would be hopeless. His brain raced. How could he convince the court of his innocence? There was such a prejudice against the American colonists, now that they were starting to humiliate the redcoats.

The turning was close where they must leave Drury Lane and swing right for the last few yards to Bow Street. Suddenly he heard racing footsteps behind them. The constables heard them too, paused, and stared back into the darkness.

A man's voice shouted, in a commanding tone, 'Stop, gentlemen! There's been a mistake.' It was the voice of authority.

'Better, I suppose,' growled the senior constable. 'He sounds as if he's somebody. With a voice like that.' They waited, the other constable keeping his tight hold on Dan's arm.

Dan knew that voice. The voice of a formidable, top-ranking gentleman – the voice that Jessica could put on so convincingly when her role required it . . .

The racing footsteps slowed. She appeared out of the gloom. 'Let this man go,' she panted. 'There's been a mistake.'

'Beg pardon, sir. We must sort it out when we get to Bow Street. We have our orders.'

'You have *my* orders, now. Let him go, you. Or I'll blow your brains out.' The younger constable's rough grip loosened promptly. His hand fell away. Dan stepped a pace to one side. There was something persuasive about the brace of pistols levelled at them.

The senior man resumed his protest. Jessica did not argue. Dan found one of the pistols thrust into his hand. 'Cover the other man,' she said. He obeyed. 'Now,' she said in a slightly more relaxed tone. 'Sit.' She might have been training a couple of dogs. 'Take your boots off.' They gaped at her. 'Go on,' she said irritably. 'Take your boots off – both of you. And if anyone asks you why you did, you can answer that if you hadn't you'd both have had your brains blown out. And, I can promise you, you would.'

She had fully recovered her breath now. The note of command in her voice was impressive. 'We'd better,' the senior man instructed his comrade. They crouched in the gutter, unlacing their ponderous boots.

From the corner of her mouth the girl murmured directions to Dan. 'We *must* keep together. I'll lead, you follow. Be ready.'

Still holding her pistol firmly in one hand she strode over to where the constables sat amid the filth and litter of the road. She picked up two of their boots and flung them, with all her strength, into the darkest shadows. The other two went crashing after them.

'Now!' she gasped, and streaked away. He followed.

Those boots had been an inspiration. Their youth would anyhow have given them a great advantage over the older policeman. But the precious minute required to recover their footwear and lace it up again was just what the young couple needed to escape from sight.

There were few people about at this late hour. And those who were seemed wrapped up in their own affairs, not in the least anxious to interfere in other people's. Had Jessica been noticeably female, someone might have intervened to help her. But the spectacle of one young man apparently chasing another was better ignored.

Half an hour later they realised, regretfully, that they had raced past the Devil without thought of the supper they had promised themselves there. Instead, they had rushed across Fleet Street and into the unsavoury district of Alsatia, for ages the criminal quarter and still an area where only the boldest of constables cared to penetrate.

'I thought a boat went from here?' she panted. 'You said the ship was moored just below the bridge?'

'It is.'

They found a belated waterman at Whitefriars Stairs and asked him to land them on the Surrey side, as near as possible upstream from London Bridge.

At last they could talk calmly. The old waterman was either deaf or pretended to be, as was tactful with a youthful pair of passengers at that late hour. He was clearly not misled by Jessica's breeches.

'You saved my life,' Dan whispered. And showed his gratitude so vigorously that she pushed him gently away.

'We need our lips for talking,' she said apologetically.

'I never dreamed you could run like that.'

She laughed. 'I haven't, since a child. So far or so fast! But a girl may need to, sometimes.'

'We're safe now.'

'But, Dan – I am worried. How can you come back to England if this is still hanging over you? You were under arrest. Till you escaped.'

'I was rescued. By a beautiful stranger!'

'This isn't a joke. It will be a shadow hanging over us.'

He tried to reassure her. The Home Office could not have tested Digby's absurd allegations. The government was so eager to win popularity – to boast that they had caught an American spy. But not so keen to admit that they had lost him again in the half-mile walk from the theatre to the lock-up! So long as Dan made himself scarce for a little while, it would suit them better to forget the whole silly business.

'Have a word with Mr Sheridan,' he suggested.

'*He* knows how innocent people can have their names blackened by malicious scandal – his play shows it. He has lots of high-up friends in government circles. He can show them that an actor's busy life doesn't offer much chance to sneak round collecting military and naval secrets.'

'I'll do my best.'

'But don't say anything to involve yourself,' he insisted.

They disembarked on Bankside, paid off the waterman and walked towards the bridge. He would not even know where they were heading. Even at this late hour, they ran into a street-seller peddling hot meat pies among the all-night workers. They bought two and devoured them ravenously, to compensate for the farewell supper they had had to miss at the Devil tavern.

Just beyond the bridge they found the Dutch vessel, *De Bloem*, alive with lights and voices in these last hours before departure.

They were shown the door of the cabin Dan was to share with two Dutch gentlemen, but he declined to disturb their slumbers. Busy though everyone seemed, a quiet word and a generous tip brought two platefuls of reasonable food and two glasses of wine to send after their meat pies. They spent the precious last two hours whispering in a shadowy corner of the deck.

'How will you get back?' he asked anxiously.

'I'll cross the bridge and walk home through the city.'

'You'll be all right?'

'Of course. It's only a mile or two. It will be broad daylight by then, the world waking up and going about its business. I'll just be another youth off to work. And I *am* armed!'

'That reminds me.' He handed back the property pistol and she slipped it into her pocket.

'I got that idea', she reminded him, 'from an enterprising young man I met at Bath.'

'I shall write to you,' he promised, 'care of the theatre. I shall word it very carefully, as if it came from some member of the audience. I'll sign it, "*your distant admirer*". Most accurate! And I'll work things out so that you can write back to me.' Though he was bound for Amsterdam, he said he would probably make for Paris as soon as he landed.

How long would they be parted? That was the merciless question they could never forget. He remained an optimist. The English would never beat a man like Washington; they would tire of the war as it became more and more hopeless.

Dan would have been even more optimistic if

he could have foreseen the developments of the next few months. In October, Burgoyne would suffer a smashing defeat at Saratoga, with thousands of redcoats surrendering. France and, afterwards Holland, would come into the war against Britain.

The darkness would pass as – quite literally – it was passing now on the deck of *De Bloem*, 'the flower' in Dutch. Strident voices rang across the deck: 'All ashore that's goin' ashore!' They said their goodbyes in a sheltered corner, so as not to attract laughter from any witnesses. Dan had bought her a little ring the afternoon before, and luckily guessed the size correctly. Hastily assuming a manly stride, Jessica hurried down the gangplank.

She stayed on the wharf till the anchor came up and the towropes tightened, drawing the ship inch by inch into the stream. He stood in the stern, waving back at her until they could no longer see each other. Then he turned and walked forward. And suddenly the whole eastern sky was brilliant with the pink and gold glory of the dawn.

I came over here, he thought, to follow a dream. And I'll come back, he vowed, for another.

Author's Note

How much is true? Some may want to know. As usual, story and central characters are made up, but the rest is as true as careful research can make it. Especially about the original Bath Theatre Royal and the shining new city then going up around it. And the history of the London theatre in Drury Lane. Many of the characters are taken from life, not only the famous ones, Sheridan and Garrick, Dr Johnson and Boswell, but all Dan and Jessica's fellow actors at Drury Lane (except the deplorable Digby) as well as Palmer and Henderson (manager and leading man at Bath), Reddish at Bristol, and even the unbelievable, talent-spotting Bate, the Fighting Parson, who appears in the *Dictionary of National Biography* under his full real name of Henry Bate Dudley. The American news in Mr Carnaby's letters was genuine. So even were Palmer's huge 'caterpillars'.

GT
BATH 1996

NIGHT PEOPLE

Maggie Pearson

All her life they seemed to have been running away.

Jools and her father Chas are always on the move. Until they reach a town where Chas has a past, and where he'd like his daughter to have a future.

While Chas plays his beloved jazz, Jools explores the strange world into which they have stepped. A world of night people. And then, one by one, the murders start.

Sinister forces are unleashed, but does Jools know where the real danger lies?

A haunting story of love and vampires . . .

COMPANIONS OF THE NIGHT

Vivian Vande Velde

A terrifying journey through the night draws Kerry to the stranger, Ethan, as they flee his vicious hunters . . .

But then the pursuers turn pursued and Kerry must choose where true danger lies – with her companion of the night – or his attackers?

A vampire seeking vengeance.

A gripping supernatural tale.

Another Hodder Children's book

THE BLOODING

Patricia Windsor

Night forest, this is where I belong. My humanness has scampered away. Now I know the happiness of the hunt.

Maris can't wait to start her summer job as an au pair in England. Life with the family seems peaceful at first. Though the children's father is unpredictable, with a wild light behind his eyes.

Sinister transformations wake Maris from her dream, and plunge her into a night-mare. A nightmare in which she must decide whether being blooded is what she really wants . . .

A stunning gothic novel.